D1250332

THE OLD WORLD

and Other Stories

ALSO BY THE AUTHOR

Novels

A Bird's Eye
Valentine's Fall
The Mermaid of Paris
The Doctor's House
Felix Roth
Sleeping Weather
The Animals' Waltz

Short Fiction

My Life Among the Apes
The Little Black Dress: Tales from France
History Lessons

Nonfiction

*City Hall and Mrs. God: A Passionate Journey
Through a Changing Toronto*

THE OLD WORLD

and Other Stories

CARY FAGAN

Copyright © 2017 Cary Fagan

Published in Canada and in the USA in 2017 by House of Anansi Press Inc.
www.houseofanansi.com

All rights reserved. No part of this publication may be reproduced or transmitted
in any form or by any means, electronic or mechanical, including photocopying,
recording, or any information storage and retrieval system, without permission
in writing from the publisher.

All of the events and characters in this book are fictitious, and any resemblance
to actual persons, living or dead, is purely coincidental.

Every reasonable effort has been made to trace ownership of copyright
materials. The publisher will gladly rectify any inadvertent errors or omissions in
credits in future editions.

House of Anansi Press is committed to protecting our natural environment.
As part of our efforts, the interior of this book is printed on paper that contains
100% post-consumer recycled fibres, is acid-free, and is processed chlorine-free.

21 20 19 18 17   1 2 3 4 5

Library and Archives Canada Cataloguing in Publication

Fagan, Cary, author
The old world and other stories / Cary Fagan.

ISBN 978-1-4870-0146-9 (paperback)

I. Title.

PS8561.A375O43 2017   C813'.54   C2016-906002-0

Library of Congress Control Number 2016958335

Cover and text design: Alysia Shewchuk
Cover image: Unknown

Canada Council   Conseil des Arts
for the Arts   du Canada

ONTARIO ARTS COUNCIL
CONSEIL DES ARTS DE L'ONTARIO
an Ontario government agency
un organisme du gouvernement de l'Ontario

We acknowledge for their financial support of our publishing program
the Canada Council for the Arts, the Ontario Arts Council, and the Government of
Canada through the Canada Book Fund.

Printed and bound in Canada

MIX
Paper from
responsible sources
FSC
www.fsc.org   FSC® C004071

For Rebecca, now and always

CONTENTS

AUTHOR'S NOTE

Many years ago the photographs in this book became separated from their original owners, faces unrecognized, settings a mystery. They floated through this world, as if on a sorrowful wind.

Of course there are millions of such images, but these thirty-five have found their way to me. I have given them stories to replace the ones they have lost. And while the stories are as varied as the photographs themselves, I imagine them belonging to one history, found in an album that might belong to any of us.

ADULTS

I T WAS THE FIRST ADULT PARTY I EVER HELD, ALTHOUGH
we weren't really adults, not quite. But it was the end of
high school, when everything would change and we all
knew it and so I desperately wanted to mark it in some
way—not by getting drunk at the lake, or racing in some
boy's car, or just by the graduation ceremony and the
dance that would follow. I wanted a party of my own,
where people would act civilized and talk about interesting things and we would see in ourselves the women and
men we were about to become.

At least that's how I see it now, all these decades later,
when I'd be surprised if a stranger could look at me and
see the girl I was then. I wanted a new pretty hairstyle and
shoes with heels. I wanted to greet people at the door and
play records just for listening and eat finger sandwiches
and say "Do you remember five years ago when we were
kids?" and "I think politics is a worthwhile career" and

"Don't you agree that Nat King Cole was a better pianist than a singer?" I wanted to make a list of who should come and who I felt obliged to ask, and revise it over and over, and spend evenings sewing my new dress with my mother nearby to help with the hard parts. I wanted to spend the afternoon of the party in the kitchen with my two best friends, Matilda and Elizabeth, cutting up celery and making dips and laughing as we spread icing on the cake, which would be cut into squares. I wanted to beg my father to let us have punch, something with a little alcohol in it, and he would pretend to be scandalized (as if he didn't know that everyone drank) but finally give in and then insist on making it himself because nobody could possibly make punch the way he could.

And I wanted every moment, every second of the party to be vivid and alive, and for it to go past midnight when my friends would help me clean up and then Dad would drive them home, and afterwards I would lie in bed, absolutely unable to sleep, smiling about something I said, or somebody else said, or how that drink got spilled and people bent to clean it up and how grown up everyone acted and how full my heart was, not with being scared as it had been for weeks now but with a most wonderful, wonderful feeling.

And it happened. It happened in just the way I imagined except that everything was the littlest bit disappointing. Choosing the guests, picking the dress pattern, making the sandwiches — all of it felt flat, no matter how I tried. Mattie and Liza didn't seem to feel that way, and I didn't know what was wrong with me, whether I had just spent too long imagining it or could never live in the moment but was always stuck inside my own head, but whatever the reason it was making me feel worse by the minute.

We dressed for the party and then waited, and of course George Francey arrived first and immediately began to tell stupid jokes. Then two more came and three after that and then a rush. I remember we were standing in the vestibule, because a few people were still coming. My father had poured us all punch, and we stood there chatting, polite and self-conscious. I could hear people in the living room talking about the Soviet Union and Elvis Presley, and it sounded just as phony as could be. I had a sudden urge to run upstairs to my room and shut the door and throw myself on the bed and cry.

And then Justine came in, and the sight of her raised my spirits a little because she's just that sort of person. Behind her came her cousin, slowly and reluctantly, stooping the way tall boys can sometimes when they're embarrassed by their height. Justine hadn't wanted to bring him but had telephoned at the last moment to ask because he was visiting for the weekend and really, she said, he was all right, a nice-as-pie farm boy who didn't know a lick about town living. Justine started telling some story and for a full two minutes forgot to introduce him. And her cousin just stood behind her, looking as if he wanted to disappear into the wallpaper, but finally she remembered, and I held out my hand and said I was glad he could come. He looked up at me (his eyes had been on his shoes), and then he didn't look away and we made just the most unimportant small talk and I felt something open inside me.

My father brought the new guests punch and then asked Justine's cousin a few questions about how the crops were looking so far, and then he and my mother took themselves upstairs and everyone breathed a sigh of relief. Voices became more relaxed, and people laughed, and we all moved into the living-dining area. Suddenly the conversations sounded real and smart and funny, and I moved around the room, spending time with this person or that, being part of a group or circle and moving on again, and I couldn't have said what was different, what had lifted the grey film from my eyes. I didn't talk to Justine's cousin, but I caught sight of him from time to time, standing in a corner examining a little porcelain figurine, or slowly eating from a bowl of cut-up fruit as if hoping it might last all night, or lingering just outside a group of boys talking about the past football season.

It must have been eleven o'clock when I found him on the front porch. Everyone who wanted to smoke went into the back yard where there was a picnic table, so he was alone. He started when he saw me and apologized and said he was looking at the moon. It was almost a full moon and would be in another day, he said, and so we looked at it together, which I thought was as corny as anything. Crickets chirped in the dark. I asked him about his plans, and he said he was going to attend veterinary school and afterwards wanted to come back to the area and serve the farmers. He was especially interested in looking after horses, although of course it was mostly going to be cows and pigs and sheep. And then he asked about me and I talked about teachers' college and how I'd always liked being with little kids and how I'd run a Sunday school and had volunteered at the library, and he said that he could see how kids would like me, which I considered pure flattery. We had about a half hour on that porch before Mattie stuck her head out and said we ought to serve cake, and I said just two minutes, and Justine's cousin took that time to ask if he could come and see me the next afternoon and perhaps we could go for a walk, and I said yes, that would be nice.

And here I am now, here *we* are, and I'm old and you're old, only you're asleep and I'm inside my head once more, thinking about how it's all gone by. Thinking how I haven't had enough of those moments, moments full of feeling like I had standing on that porch with you, that there was always too much day-to-day, just getting breakfast on the table and the kids onto the bus, and then heading off to work and back home to make dinner, and falling dead tired into bed. And I know what you'd say if you were awake, you'd say that I worry too much, that I'm too much of a brooder, as I've always been, and that we've got more life ahead of us, and we're going to make the most of it, every second. And I want to believe you, my tall, awkward, nice-as-pie farm boy, even if I'm the sort of person who never quite does.

THE CALL

I WAIT.

I am waiting.

Yes, I am waiting for the telephone to ring, which it will do at precisely 10:30 this morning. So I have been told. "Expect a call at precisely ten thirty. Be sure to answer it promptly. It is of utmost importance."

I responded in the affirmative, saluted, and turned quickly to march-step back to my desk. In seven years I have never been told to expect a call. Of course the telephone has rung. Of course I have answered it. A higher-up will make a demand, a subordinate a request, placing into my lap some problem to be solved or, perhaps, sent into permanent limbo. This is what I am good at, why I've lasted for seven years in the same position, at this desk where it is warm, where nobody tries to shoot me, where lunch breaks occur at the same time every day and from my briefcase I take out the paper bag with the small meal prepared for me by my Anna. More than once I've heard them say about me: "Now that fellow, he knows what to do with a problem. He's reliable and you can depend on him to make sure it won't raise its head again. Give it to him and he'll send it to another department, or wrap it up in requests for information, or demand local and regional interpretations that will never be given." And when I am praised to my face I never take credit but instead say, "But I am only following the protocols already established," and everyone will nod as if they know just what I am talking about.

And yet here I am, told to receive a call at precisely 10:30. What can this mean? I was informed of it by the colonel just as I came in at nine, and I have been waiting for an hour and eighteen minutes. It is a good thing that I set my watch by the radio while Anna was packing my lunch this morning. The strange thing is, my telephone has not rung once yet, when three or four times is the norm. Has my line been cleared to receive this one important call? Is there a reason for the advance notice, for the exact specification of time? Have I been chosen to receive this call instead of one of the other officers at the other desks in the other tiny rooms?

Don't worry, I tell myself. *You have done nothing wrong.* But is that really true? Have I done nothing wrong in seven years? I think back and remember this or that little incident, a smudging of a signature, a misplacing of a medical report, a box of cigars or other small token accepted. Yet wasn't I keeping within the spirit of my position? Didn't I give that box of cigars to the colonel? Surely these small irregularities are not worth remarking on. Surely I have amply satisfied those above me. Does not everyone like me? Haven't I been careful to make no enemies?

Doom. That's what I feel — absolute and inevitable doom.

If only there was something to take my mind off waiting. On my desk are several papers placed there to make me look busy. Also a little box given to me from Anna that, when opened, makes a noise like a cricket. Also a book lent to me by the colonel, who expects me to like it as much as he did. Slipped inside is the invitation from him and his wife to their anniversary party, an invitation that I worked quietly to obtain by further ingratiating myself. I was so delighted to receive it that I bent the rules that day and used my telephone to call Anna with the news. And of course she was thrilled and immediately began to plan what to contribute to the buffet table, as well as to devise a list of conversation topics that she might engage in with the colonel's wife, who is notoriously difficult.

Only one paper on my desk disturbs me at all. It is not official correspondence but a letter from my father. I haven't answered this letter, nor do I have any intention of answering it, just as I have not responded to any of his letters over the last three years. I will never forgive my father, no matter how many letters he sends. I consider him dead. In this one he writes: *Will you never forgive me? Will you continue to ignore my existence, to refuse a father's love for his son?* Empty words! That I haven't thrown it out already shows only a remaining streak of sentimentality. But I will throw it out, have no doubt of that.

I check my watch. It is 10:27. In three minutes I will receive the call. I wonder how best to answer it. Usually I simply say my name. If the call is likely coming from within the department I might say "Desk three!" Occasionally I employ a simple good morning or afternoon. But I'm not sure what's appropriate here, and there's nothing worse than indecision.

In two minutes the telephone will ring.

Another lucky thing is that Anna ironed my uniform last night. I myself polished the buttons and waxed the leather straps. I've never understood how the officer at desk two can present himself in so slovenly a fashion, as if he feels no respect for our duties and no need to project an air of competency and firmness. I wouldn't be surprised if the colonel reprimanded him; you can be sure *he* received no invitation to the anniversary party. I remember as if it were yesterday the first time I put on this uniform. How strange it felt, and when I looked in the mirror I saw a man taller, more handsome, more commanding than myself. And now after seven years I have become that man. What if this call, for reasons I don't even know, results in my uniform being taken from me? Who will I be then?

The telephone rings. The usual two short rings — did I expect something different? For some reason I look at my watch and see that it is twenty seconds before 10:30.

I put my hand on the receiver and...hesitate.

It rings again. What on earth am I doing! Why didn't I pick it up right away?

It rings again. I snatch up the receiver, fumble it, press it to my ear. "Good afternoon. I mean, good morning! This is desk, ah, this is desk *three!*"

"Are you all right?"

"Who is that? Anna?"

"Of course it's me. You sound peculiar."

"Why are you calling? You know this number is off limits except for emergencies."

"Yes, but you yourself called me on it about the party. I wanted to ask what you thought of my bringing a fish casserole. Everyone always raves about it, that is if they like fish, but I don't know the tastes of the colonel or his wife—"

"I cannot speak about this now! Do you hear me!"

"There's no need to shout."

"I am expecting a call!"

"You're expecting a call? What sort of call? Should I be worried? Did you do something wrong?"

"This is not a gossip line! I will speak to you at home!"

I hang up the receiver. Sweat has broken out on my brow and I take out my handkerchief to wipe it away. I look at my watch. It is 10:31. It is one minute past the time I was to expect the call.

I wait.

The telephone remains mute. I wait longer. Nothing. The time is now 10:33. Is it possible that the expected call

15

could not get through because I was speaking to Anna? It can't be!

Snatching up the receiver, I check for the dial tone. Yes, it's there. I put it down again.

Ten minutes crawl by. A half hour. And then it is almost noon. A disaster! I fold my arms and lay my head down on them.

A rap on the door frame causes me to jerk up again. It is the colonel. I stand and salute.

"Not sleeping, are you?"

"No, sir."

"I trust you received the call?"

"The call, sir?"

"Yes, the call that was to come at ten thirty."

"Of course. Of course I did. I received it precisely on time as expected."

"And?"

I look at the colonel, at his small blue eyes and shining pate. "May I ask, sir, if you know the nature of the call?"

"Not precisely."

"Well, rest assured, Colonel, that everything is taken care of. No need to trouble yourself at all."

The colonel smiled. "Excellent. To be honest, that's something of a relief. Once more you've done first-rate work." He turns to go, stops, and half turns back. "And you've got the invitation to our little soiree?"

"I certainly do!"

"Now, if anyone is looking for me, I've gone to the club for lunch."

"Yes, sir."

I salute once more as the colonel leaves. I feel my heart smacking my ribs. With the tips of my fingers I touch my own face. Yes, I am still here. *Calm down*, I tell myself. I sit again and, opening my briefcase, take out the paper-bag lunch prepared by Anna. I open the bag and lay out a napkin and, on top of it, a devilled egg, a small glass jar of herring, a package of crisps. I begin to eat. And when I am done I put the remains back into the paper bag and the bag into my briefcase.

I look at the letter on my desk.

From another desk drawer I take a sheet of paper. I pick up my pen.

Dear Father, I begin.

FORTUNE

THERE WASN'T MUCH LUCK IN MY LIFE. TWENTY-TWO years old, living in the same room I'd been born in, eating my mother's cooking (stew on Monday, corn fritters on Tuesday, fish casserole on Wednesday), working behind the counter at Podnacks' Pharmacy making Coke floats and vanilla shakes and egg creams for the kids crowding in when the high school let out, the same as I myself was doing a few years before. Mr. Podnacks was fair enough but he was a stern s.o.b. Always the professional with his white smock and the pens clipped in his pocket and the precise movements of his fat little hands. His kingdom was among the powders and other hocus-pocus behind the pharmacy counter, and God forbid I should ever set foot back there.

Then there was Mrs. Podnacks, who sat at the cash register filing her nails or reading a magazine from the rack. She was a good fifteen years younger than

Mr. Podnacks, whose first wife had claimed he was trying to poison her and ended up in the state institution. The new Mrs. Podnacks was always showing off her gams and then giving me a look if she saw me glance her way. And there was Ralph who made the deliveries, showing off on his bicycle around town, always taking his sweet time to get back. So there's me, who dreamed of seeing the world, stuck forever in this two-bit town, and everyone else happy for me to remain here until they put me in the ground. Made me choke so that I couldn't breathe.

So that's why I made my plan to leave. I didn't have much money saved, having to pay my father for my room and board, but I got an old duffle bag to hold my clothes and a new chipboard case for my guitar. And because I had to tell somebody, I let my little brother Kyle in on it. We shared a room anyway and as we lay in bed I told him how I would hop a freight train and work my way west, where the weather was fine and you could pick a new life as easily as an orange from a tree. How I would have adventures and make my fortune. Of course I'd have to make some money along the way, picking up a day's work here and there. Mostly I hoped to earn my keep with my voice and my guitar. I could find a restaurant or bar that would hire me, maybe even one of those radio shows, and if worst came to worst I could stand on a street corner and open my case.

Kyle listened to me practice: Carter Family and Jimmy Rogers and especially Frank Hutchison, with his fine guitar-picking on "Worried Blues" and "The Train that

Carried the Girl from Town." Kyle sometimes even sang harmony with me. He had an angelic voice. He said with my talent I was sure to make out good, and even though he was just a kid I was glad to hear it.

Even once I'd decided, I stayed around, for much as I burned for a different life, I was afraid, too. But then one night something happened. It was after dinner and Ralph came by on his bicycle to tell me that I was wanted in the store to help with the inventory. I walked over and found the pharmacy dark but the front door open. I heard a voice call my name and walked to the back of the store, past the counter, where I'd never set foot before. There were shelves of pills and bottles and a small work table with a mortar and pestle, and also a cot in the corner. Mrs. Podnacks was sitting on the cot, long legs crossed, two buttons of her blouse undone, and as I came in she raised her eyes and gave me that look of hers.

Maybe she meant something, maybe she meant nothing. Maybe she was as bored as I was. But I turned around and ran. Ran all the way home, and that night I packed my duffle and shut the guitar in its case and got into bed with my clothes on. I told Kyle that I'd send him a postcard when I could. He got all teary while I lay staring up at the low ceiling trying to imagine what lay ahead. Finally I fell asleep, only to wake up a few hours later. I looked at my watch, but it was cheap and I didn't trust it. I grabbed my stuff and climbed out the window.

It was eerie walking through the silent town and then past the train station to a stand of birch trees where I hid. There were already a couple of men waiting there in the dark, hungry eyed and with patched clothes, but not unfriendly. The 705 chugged into the station, stopped about three minutes to unload the mail-order, and then slowly pulled out again. The other men waited for a car with an open door and then they were running. They hopped up easily and called for me to hurry. I handed one my gear and the other pulled me in as the train picked up speed. They patted me on the back and one of the men took a flat bottle out of his jacket and said we should make a toast to the "first-timer."

This was the sort of camaraderie I had hoped to find on the road. I had taken some food from the kitchen, slices of cooked ham and half a loaf of bread and some peaches, and now I shared it around. We began feeling pretty content with our bellies full and the soothing rattle of the train. The man with the bottle asked if I'd take out my guitar and grace them with a song. I was only too happy to oblige.

I unlatched the case and opened it up and found inside nothing but a towel wrapped around a couple of stones.

We hadn't even passed the first town yet and already I was robbed, already I was ruined. And in that instant I knew. My little brother Kyle. That little shit had taken it out while I was sleeping. He'd always envied that guitar and sometimes I'd caught him sitting on my bed with it, working out the chords. No doubt he would soon be singing "Little Darling Pal of Mine" while I hurtled toward God knows where.

WE HAVE TO BE CAREFUL

Excuse me, buddy, you work here?

Certainly, sir. What can I do for you?

I saw the sign in the window.

Of course. You're interested in blankets, then? We have some beautiful models. Naturally there are the classic wool blankets, very traditional, just two pastel stripes, warm as anything. Some people do find wool a little itchy, but with a nice cotton top sheet...

I didn't say nothing about sheets.

No, that's very true. We also have our new line of synthetic blankets, made of Norcron. Have you heard of it?

Can't say I have.

Wonderful space-age stuff. Light and silky, but also warm. And all kinds of patterns—stars, squares, even teddy bears and trains for the kids. Here, just feel this— soft, yes?

I'll say.

27

Comes in eight colours, a decorator's dream. Of course some people always prefer what's traditional, and we certainly do have cold winters here. But personally I'm gung ho for the new synthetics. I don't like the weight on my feet. Believe me, it won't be long before your neighbours have them.

I ain't planning on sleeping in my neighbour's bed.

No, certainly, ha ha, I didn't mean to suggest you were.

Tell me about the lay-a-way. It's like paying on the instalment plan, right?

Not exactly. You give us a deposit—even five dollars is enough—and we will reserve the item or items you want. You make regular payments until the full amount is reached, and then you take your purchase home. It's interest free, and you don't end up in debt. For example, if you change your mind we'll return all the money you've deposited with us to date.

Deposited? You sound like a friggin' bank.

Well, at Gates we believe that we're just as reliable.

It's a funny-sounding term, don't you think?

I don't follow.

Say it over fast. Layaway, layaway, layaway.

Perhaps you'd like to browse a while and I can come back to you.

You got any other layaway plans at the moment? Any other *items*, I mean.

Not that I am aware of.

You sure about that? Because I heard otherwise. I heard tell of making a deposit on a person. And then you add to it every week until that person comes home with you.

We don't sell people at Gates, sir. Now if you'll excuse me—

But I know for a fact you do.

I'm sure I have no idea what you mean. Please let go of my jacket. I really will have to call security.

I've got a friend, he bought himself a twelve-year-old boy here just last week. Took him almost eight months to make the payments. Now he's got that kid shovelling coal from a truck.

This really isn't funny. You're making me very uneasy. My advice is that you leave right now.

And a woman who's on my bowling team. She bought herself an old fellow to read to her at night. He didn't cost so much, on account of him having only a few good years left.

Now sir, I am asking you once and only once. What is it you want?

I want a layaway person, that's all.

You aren't the police?

Do I look like it?

May I see some identification, please.

Here's my wallet.

We have to be careful. Yes, this looks in order. Please follow me to the back.

Not a lot of shoppers today, by the looks of it.

Mondays are slow. Just through this door and down the corridor.

Lead the way.

Here we are. Watch it, this door's heavy. After you.

Well, I'll be. You'd never suspect if you didn't know. How many you got here? Thirty?

Thirty-six. It fluctuates, of course. Some are returned, others go out. At one point last year we fell to seven. Problem with supply. There's no coercion, you see. You can't just scoop people up.

They look comfortable enough here, playing cards and so forth. Is that a buffet table?

We have regular meals, of course, but yes, the buffet is constantly replenished.

What's behind the glass door?

A swimming pool and gymnasium. And there's a stairway to the roof garden. But if we can get down to business, what — or should I say *who* — are you looking for?

I need a woman about my age or a little younger. She don't have to be beautiful but pleasant-looking would be nice. Easy with the small talk, for parties and such. With some class, is what I'm saying. You see, I'm getting pressure at work, not being married, and I need somebody to step out with. There are a lot of social occasions for my work, out-of-town customers, cocktails, a few formal affairs. I got a small house with an extra bedroom set up. Other than the social events, she can pretty much do what she likes, although if she enjoys cooking that would be a bonus. I wouldn't mind company once in a while in front of the TV or even a game of Scrabble.

Yes, yes, good, not excessively demanding. You have

been admirably precise, which makes my job much easier. I'll just consult the register. Hmm. We have two who would fit the bill. One — she's at the organ in the corner — is a little more because of her musical ability. You can see the amount here. The other — she's the redhead laughing at the card table — is just a little older but with a warm personality. She does have a limp. You can see the amount is a good twenty percent less.

I'm partial to redheads. And the limp is a bonus — it'll bring out a sympathetic feeling in people. They'll think well of me.

You are just the sort of customer we like, someone who understands the value of our service.

I'll take her.

Excellent. What can you put down?

I've got fifty dollars.

That's fine. And remember, you can come in and make a payment any time. If you're careful she can be on your arm at one of those social occasions before you know it.

While we're at it, I could use a new set of blankets for her bed. Let's do a layaway on that, too.

Even better. What do you think, wool or synthetic?

How about we ask her. After all, she'll be sleeping under them.

Very thoughtful, sir. Very thoughtful.

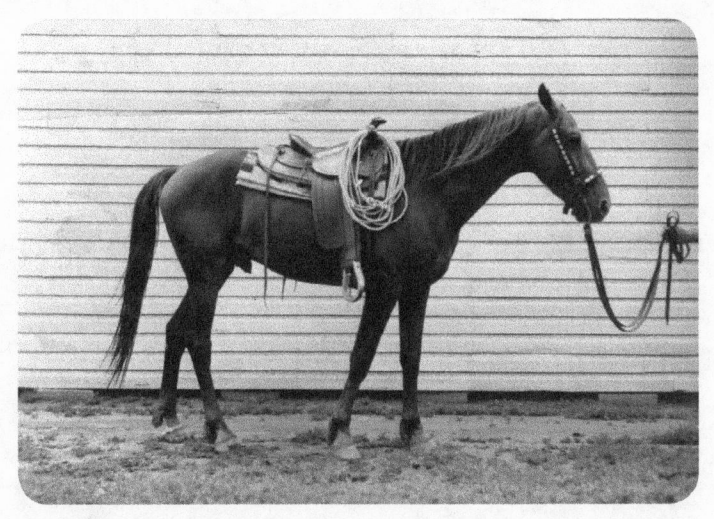

JUMP

"**D**ON'T YOU WORRY. PRINCE IS AS GENTLE AS A lamb."

He tapped his cigarette on his heel. I knew he was trying to make me look like the lesser man. I had never ridden in my life and he knew it. And either way he would win. I could refuse and look pathetic or I could accept and be thrown to the ground and probably get my head cracked open. Why he had it out for me was pretty obvious. Maureen.

The horse stamped its foot. "Prince is wanting a little exercise. He hasn't had a rider in two days. I already put a new blanket and saddle on him. What do you say?"

Maureen put her hand on my arm. She knew very well what her touch did to me. "You don't have to." She might as well have said, *I understand if you're a coward who chooses to be humiliated.* She gave me her charmingly ironic smile.

I was a city boy and had never liked climbing, rowing, or games of any sort. But it wasn't a particularly big horse, and it was rather handsome, with a dark, contemplative eye. Of course I'd read a lot of books in which men rode horses. They threw themselves on, grabbed the reins, yelled "Giddy-up!" and hit the spurs. For them it was always a piece of cake. I took a step toward the horse.

"So what's her name again?"

He chuckled knowingly. "She's a *he*. Prince."

I took another step. "Good boy, Prince."

"You put your foot in the stirrup," Maureen said helpfully.

"Right." I raised my foot, trying not to lose my balance, and got it hooked in.

"Your *other* foot," she said. "Unless you want to ride facing backwards."

I struggled to get free and then put my other foot in. I grasped the leather horn on the saddle and jerked myself up. The horse swayed a bit and shook his head. The saddle felt all right under me, warm and smooth.

He tossed me the reins.

"Hold them like this," he said, shortening them up.

"You look good up there," Maureen said.

Her words made my fear almost worth it. I gave her a comical smile and a little wave. If only somebody would lead me around, like a kid on a pony ride, I might enjoy myself.

"Just stay on the track," Maureen said. "Once or twice around."

"Yes, ma'am," I said, touching an invisible stetson. I looked straight ahead and shook the reins.

The horse didn't move.

"Come on, little dogie," I said, giving a kick with my heels.

"Dogies are cows," he said. "Why don't I get you started."

"No, that's all right, I'm sure I'll get—"

Prince took off.

I was thrown backwards so hard it felt like whiplash. I had to grab hold of the horn, which meant letting go of the reins. The horse thundered along the path that led to the track. His hooves pounded on the packed ground. I bumped painfully up and down, sure I'd be flung off. The track curved around but the horse kept going straight, heading straight up the hill instead. Maureen yelled something. The hill slowed him a little, which allowed me to lean forward and fish for the flapping reins, but then he was on the other side and speeding up again.

And then I saw the fence.

It was a classic white farm fence with a gate, which was closed. On the other side several cows stopped grazing to look up at us. *Don't jump, please don't jump.* But the gate was coming up fast and there was no way to stop and so instead I yelled "Jump!" just in case Prince obeyed verbal commands like a circus animal.

It wasn't that he obeyed me; he just didn't want to hit the fence, either. His ears flattened and we rose into the air. My heart jammed up in my throat. We soared over and came down to earth on the other side with such a thud that I slid sideways, just managing to hold on and pull myself back up.

The cows scattered, bellowing mournfully as we passed. Why wouldn't the damn horse slow down? For one thing, he seemed to like running on the short grass. It was hard for me to look far ahead and so I didn't see the other fence until we were almost on it. I had a split second to embrace the terror before we were in the air again.

Prince's back hoof clanged on the top rail. It felt like an electric jolt running up my spine. He galloped on steadily, finding his stride again. Leaning forward the way I'd seen jockeys do, I heard the rhythmic and powerful huff from his wide nostrils. "Okay, that's a good horse," I said in a voice more strained than soothing. Now the ground was scrubby, with rocks or gravel strewn about. I made myself look up and saw trees rising. I remembered Maureen talking about the large forest that spread north.

Prince passed the first trees and moved along a narrow but clear path. We were trotting. Every so often an evergreen branch brushed my shoulder. The trees blotted out much of the light, and the air was heavy with pollen or wood particles or something. The path began to rise until we were on a ridge with the forest falling away on either side and I could appreciate how beautiful it was. With the reins in my hands I sat more upright. It occurred to me that if I pulled on the reins I might be able to get Prince to stop.

I didn't pull on the reins.

Ahead was a bed of pine needles dappled with light. A fox turned its narrow head to us and passed into the trees. "You're something else, Prince," I whispered, and he raised his head as if acknowledging the compliment. I realized that I wasn't scared anymore.

The trees thinned and we emerged onto a path that ran along a field of sunflowers on heavy stalks. We moved alongside their intoxicating colour for a good mile before Prince turned down a slope. Below us was a verdant hollow with a river running along its bottom. As we moved down, the trees looked different, almost tropical, with vines winding up the trunks and dangling trumpet-shaped flowers. Before some of the blooms hovered tiny, iridescent things with blurred wings. Hummingbirds.

Prince stepped almost delicately as the ground became steep and studded with mica-inflected rocks. As he worked his way down to the riverbank, I could see that the water wasn't tranquil but swift-moving. He walked along onto the wet mud.

"Now, boy," I said, patting his neck, "we really don't need to—"

But he waded in. When my own legs began to submerge I felt an icy shock. Still Prince kept going, and we kept sinking, and I could only hope that the water wouldn't rise any higher under the horse's head.

The bottom dropped out.

We both went under and came up again, sputtering. I held onto Prince's mane as he paddled furiously. The current pulled us along; it was far too strong for the horse to break through. I wasn't sure if I had a better chance holding on or swimming on my own but it seemed as if we were in this together. I choked on mouthfuls of water. I would drown and never see Maureen or anyone I knew again. On and on the river took us until we were both limp with exhaustion. I could barely hold on while Prince's legs hardly moved. His head turned to the side and I saw his eye roll upwards.

But just then the current relaxed. The river was entering a large lake. Prince's hooves touched bottom and he stumbled onto the stony beach. For the first time the horse stood still.

"We made it, ol' boy."

Prince let me rub the side of his face. He walked onto the grass and let his head drop so that he could crop a mouthful. I let him eat. Looking ahead, I saw a green plain and mountains rising in the distance. The mountains were very old, their shapes softened by time, and all green but for one bare knob. The sun was already getting low and at some point we would have to stop and sleep, but not yet. I did think for a moment of Maureen, but I knew that Prince and I would keep moving toward the mountains.

MRS. ORGANDY, NAKED

M RS. ORGANDY APPEARED ON OUR DOORSTEP LESS than an hour after the moving van had gone, holding a baked lasagna in a glass dish and a small gathering of flowers from her garden. My mother, who had been anxious about making new acquaintances, was delighted. She insisted on introducing me and my two little sisters.

Mrs. Organdy, it turned out, was the school secretary. When school started I would see her at least once a week when I signed out to go to the doctor for my allergy injections. Maybe it was because she didn't have to keep a bunch of kids in line all day, but Mrs. Organdy was always way more cheerful than our teachers. The first time I came into the office to sign out, she asked me if the needle hurt and told me how she'd once been treated for a drooping eye. She asked me if I could tell which one it was. (I could, but I pretended otherwise.)

Mrs. Organdy wasn't the acknowledged favourite in

the school; that was the kindergarten teacher, who was beautiful and sang with a trill and who, after Christmas, didn't return because she had gotten married. Most of the girls and even some of the boys in her class cried when they heard. But still, everybody liked Mrs. Organdy. She wasn't just nice, she was *interesting*; even adults thought so. Mrs. Organdy went to unusual places for her holidays, such as Venezuela and Portugal. She was known to speak French. She was a member of the Book-of-the-Month Club and always chose an alternative selection.

Of course I saw her more than once a week, because Mrs. Organdy lived at 1220 Norfolk Street and we lived at 1218. She had a very pretty flower garden in the front yard and a small pond in the back where goldfish lived all year round, even when it iced over, and she was often on her knees working in the beds or sitting on a folding chair by the pond, reading. Mrs. Organdy didn't have children. She also didn't seem to have a Mr. Organdy, at least not one that anyone saw. I didn't think he was dead because people would have said so, and I often speculated on his whereabouts. Fighting in Korea? Saving lives as a doctor in Africa? In prison for robbing a bank? All seemed possible for someone who had married Mrs. Organdy.

Our house had three bedrooms on the second floor and my younger sisters, who were only a year apart, shared the back one. I was ten years old and also a boy so I got the small, middle bedroom to myself. The window faced Mrs. Organdy's house. I often lay on the bed and listened to my transistor radio, or sprawled on the rag rug and read comic books, or — more reluctantly — sat at my desk doing homework. It was while I was doing my math homework, about three months after we moved in, that I first saw Mrs. Organdy naked.

Until then the light had always been off in the room across from my window. But on that day it flicked on and Mrs. Organdy began to go in and out of the room, bringing in various art supplies — a three-legged easel, a stool, a pile of canvases, a wooden box of paints. She wasn't completely naked — she had a small blue scarf, or bandana, around her neck, something she occasionally wore at school. Of course it was the first time that I'd seen a woman's body and I was quite surprised by certain details. Without clothes her manner of walking, feet slightly turned out, became more pronounced.

From then on I often saw Mrs. Organdy in that room, standing before the easel with a pallet in one hand and a brush in the other. Always she wore only some little accent, a French-style beret perched at an angle on her head, a tiger-striped blanket over her shoulders. She would paint for an hour or so, frowning most of the time, and every so often a different-sized canvas would take the place of the one that had been there before. Sometimes she got paint on her thigh or arm, and once a drip of orange landed on her breast. The canvas was angled away so I had to imagine what she was painting. It occurred to me that because I could see her she ought to be able to see me, but I never saw her look my way. Even so, I made a point of closing the curtain when it came time to put on my pajamas.

Something told me not to tell my parents that Mrs. Organdy liked to paint in the nude. I thought they might find it wrong and go knock on her door and say, "I'm sure you don't realize but..." I couldn't see why a nice person like Mrs. Organdy needed to be embarrassed like that. Also, how could I then go into the office every week and ask her to sign me out?

And so I continued to do my homework at my desk, and Mrs. Organdy continued to paint. School finished at the end of June and Mrs. Organdy went away for the entire summer to France. I also went away, but just for two weeks to summer camp, which I didn't like much. I preferred just hanging around doing nothing special. Then September came and Mrs. Organdy appeared in her garden, and my mother went out to ask her what it was like in France. School started and I continued the routine of signing out for my weekly injections, even though my allergies hadn't improved.

But Mrs. Organdy didn't appear nude again. Not long after she returned from her trip she moved the easel, the stool, the canvases, and the box of paints out of the room. The thought that she was giving up her painting upset me until I realized she was probably just shifting to the other extra bedroom, the one facing her back yard, which, like my sisters', got more light. I was sorry but had to admit that it became easier to get my homework done.

One day after school, Mrs. Organdy knocked on our door. She told my mother (I was listening from the top of the stairs) that she was having a "little exhibition" of paintings at the recreation centre. There was going to be an opening party on Saturday afternoon, and she gave my mother an invitation she'd produced on the school Gestetner machine. My mother, who said she'd never been to an art opening, was quite excited and said we had to go.

I panicked. "We can't go," I insisted.

"Why not?"

"Because I want to go to the movies."

"That's not very nice, is it? I'm sure we can go to the movies another time."

"All right," said my father. "We'll go to the art show. But remember, she's just an *amateur* painter."

I think he said this just to annoy her. But I cringed at the thought of my parents seeing Mrs. Organdy's paintings. They were sure to be nudes and, who knows, they might even show her close up.

On Saturday I pretended to be sick but my mother felt my head and told me to get dressed. We dropped my sisters off at a birthday party and then drove to the recreation centre. The building smelled of chlorine from the indoor pool. There were hand-drawn signs taped to the concrete-block walls showing the way to the exhibit in the general purpose room. A lot of people were already there, standing around and holding plastic cups of Coca-Cola. Some people were looking at the paintings but a lot more were just talking to each other. I recognized the school principal and a couple of teachers but nobody else. I was the only kid.

I hung back while my parents went over to congratulate Mrs. Organdy. When they were caught up in the crowd I began to walk around the walls of the large rectangular room. At first I didn't look at the paintings but just kept walking slowly around, until finally I couldn't wait any longer and lifted my gaze.

I saw a painting of a giant chicken standing beside the Eiffel Tower.

A horse standing in a field of gigantic sunflowers.

A baby carriage next to a monstrous watermelon.

I was looking at the moon inside a teacup when I felt a hand on my shoulder. "So," Mrs. Organdy said, smiling. "What do you think?"

"They're . . . they're the best paintings I've ever seen."

I meant it. It didn't matter that I'd never been to an art gallery before — I was sure that I would like Mrs. Organdy's paintings more than any others. She gave my shoulder a squeeze. "You're an artist's dream," she said. And then my parents came over.

Of course my father didn't want to buy one, but my mother insisted. She chose the moon in the teacup. At home she propped it on a bookcase where it remained for several months. But then things began to get piled in front of it, not just books but also a vase someone had given my parents and a lopsided ceramic tree made by one of my sisters. When the painting had just about disappeared I slipped it out from behind the mess of things and took it to my room where I propped it on my dresser.

Shortly after that, Mrs. Organdy got a job in a different

school, and in the summer she went away again, only this time she didn't come back. A "For Sale" sign appeared on the lawn and one weekend in late August I watched a new family move in. They were, my mother said as she prepared brownies, the mirror opposite of us—two small boys and one older girl.

I took my hockey cards onto the porch so that I could watch the truck being unloaded. Looking up, I saw the girl, who paused to scowl at me before tromping into the house. She sure looked mad at having to move. I thought she might murder her whole family. Sorting my cards, I wondered where Mrs. Organdy had gone. Morocco, I thought, or maybe back to France. Places where she would be sure to fit in.

My mother came out holding the dish of brownies covered in aluminum foil. "What a nice day," she said. "Do you want to come next door and give these brownies with me?"

I thought of the furious girl stomping into the house. "Okay," I said, getting up.

My mother ran her fingers through my hair to brush back my bangs. I brushed them forward again as we went down the porch steps.

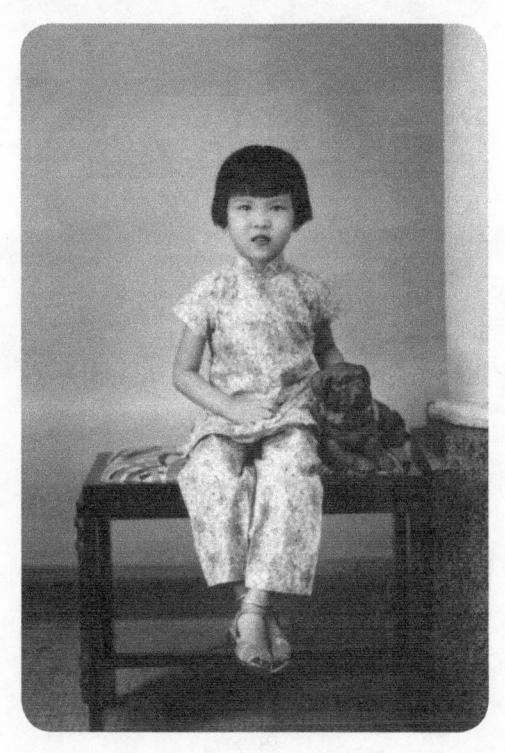

BAD WORDS

As always, I write you on the birthday of our daughter. Anisa is five years old. And as always, I send you a photograph that we had taken at the studio. You don't ask for this letter, or this photograph, I know, and you never reply. Will you answer this time? I won't hold my breath. But, still, I send it.

Anisa is, if anything, more talkative than ever. In fact, she only stops when she's asleep or crying. She is a running stream of commentary: what she's doing, what she's thinking, what she wants or doesn't want. Even what the objects around her — chair, book, stuffed animal — are thinking. If she scribbles a picture she'll ask me to admire it, and then she kisses the paper before putting it in her folder. She's an animist, our daughter — she believes that everything has a soul. You must be nice to your pillow, your hairbrush. And if you aren't nice, if you become angry and throw the hairbrush across the room, you must later pick it up and stroke it and apologize so that you will be forgiven because of course you are a good person at heart.

Isn't everybody a good person at heart? She asked me that just the other day, God knows where the phrase came from. She picks things up from everywhere. Swear words, too, which of course interest her intensely. What makes a word bad? Why is it forbidden? Where does its dark power come from? If you say it, does the word give you its power or does it hurt you? Does it make a difference if you say the word for no reason or when you're feeling as though you have a lightning storm inside? Just try to explain these sorts of things, day in and day out.

But of course, you don't have to. I wonder if you ever say to someone: "I have a daughter. Her name is Anisa and she lives on the other side of the world." Maybe it gets you sympathy, makes you seem sensitive. Or perhaps you like to think of her when you're alone, having a drink or two, letting your sentimental side come out. I hope it's not to feel sorry for us, because we certainly don't need you. It suddenly occurs to me that you might read this letter as some sort of plea for help. Well, just don't.

I've told you in the past that Anisa is unusually bright, but she has also become unusually wilful. Of course all children have tantrums, misbehave, push against the tyranny of the parent who they need and love and therefore must sometimes despise. It is often a fight to get her to do anything—to take a bath, button a jacket, settle down for sleep. When she goes to a friend's house, she never wants to leave, even if the other parents insist it's time. "I'm staying, I'm staying!" she shouts. She will lie on the floor and kick her feet or tear her own clothes or knock over glasses and dishes. More than once I've had to carry her out kicking and screaming, and believe me she isn't afraid to hurt me if she can. Often as not I'm covered in scratches and bruises. Not long ago I scooped her up, head down, hoping to break the mood and make her laugh, and she kicked me in the eye. I had to wear a patch for three weeks. Of course she felt awful and made me tell her several times a day that I forgave her, that I knew she wasn't really trying to hurt me.

She looks nice in the photograph, doesn't she? Her hair is combed, her face is washed. She sits calmly, her ankles crossed, her hand on the cast-iron dog (belonging to the photographer). But I can't tell you how much effort went into catching this one image. How she ran from me laughing, pulled off her sandals, ran back to the waiting room, then over to the window to watch a brass band, which gave her the idea of marching across the room and making noises through her lips. How this game became serious to her, as if she weren't keeping away from me for fun but because I would do something terrible to her if I caught her, how she became frantic as she hid behind the photographer's legs. How did I finally get her to co-operate? Bribery. A promise of a trip to her favourite candy store. I even gave her money — it's there, crumpled in the hand in her lap. If you look closely you can see that she isn't calm at all; she's alert, expectant, about to jump up again. All this to take a photograph for someone who's never asked for one.

I know all this must sound as if I'm complaining and feeling sorry for myself. But that isn't it at all—I'd never write you for that reason. The simple truth is that I'm thankful for Anisa every day. Because above all she's a loving child. She gives me kisses at unexpected times or climbs up when I'm reading on the sofa to lie next to me, warm as a hot water bottle. She tells me stories about talking trees and dragons and bad boys who have to be tricked. She makes up jokes with punchlines that sometimes make no sense and sometimes are unbelievably clever. She astonishes me every day with her bright thoughts and her quixotic compassion. She wants to give our money to a legless man begging on the sidewalk or comes up with a scheme for taking in all the stray cats. She asks me about my childhood and listens with deep intensity. She asks me about the world.

She also asks me about you. And I tell her, of course I do. I tell her everything good, everything to make her feel strength in who she is. But the photograph—that's for you. Because you don't know how much you've lost, how much less your life is than it could have been. I send it so that you'll at least have something to last another year.

TELL ME A SECRET

IT'S BEAUTIFUL.

Can you please get off your back?

I've never seen a more beautiful tree. Come down and look with me.

It's cold. We've been walking for almost two hours. I thought we were going to find the road and end up in a restaurant. All I can think of is soup.

The world looks different when you're gazing up. Your own life looks different.

Life looks different when you're eating a bowl of soup. Just come down here. Do it for me.

Fine. I don't want to appear unchivalrous. God, I'm not as flexible as I used to be. Is the ground actually dry? You're not lying on deer poop or anything?

It's just cold.

This is my good leather jacket.

You're vain. But I learned that about you the first time we met. Get down here already.

Okay, okay. Yup, it's a tree.

A beautiful tree. The *most* beautiful tree.

I don't know that it's more beautiful than, say, the three or four thousand other trees we've seen today. Besides, it's dead.

It isn't dead.

Clearly that's a dead tree.

It's almost winter—all the trees have lost their leaves. That's why we're lying on them. I'm quite sure you learned about the seasons at some point in your education.

That is not just a tree denuded of leaves due to the earth's path in the solar system. That's a dead tree. Look at the bark. It's peeling off. You're looking at a dead, or diseased, or possibly poisoned tree.

Whatever, it's beautiful.

You know what that's like? That's like seeing a corpse and saying, "Gee, that's the most beautiful person I ever saw."

I think it might snow today. The sky is the colour of an old pot. Snow brings peace.

It's as if you're talking in haiku today. I wish I had a pen.

Walks are good. I'm learning a lot about you. I didn't know you were quite this cynical. And insecure. Wanting to sound smart.

Oh no, the inevitable psychoanalysis. All right, I accept the diagnosis. Is this a problem for you?

It requires some adjustment.

I'll try to tone it down.

You know, this really is a good opportunity to learn something more about each other.

We're not getting up?

Not yet. Tell me something.

What kind of something?

Something about yourself I don't know. Something you don't tell people. A secret.

I don't really like games.

Don't think of it as a game. Think of it as revealing who you are. I don't mind going first. Let me think a minute. Oh, I know. When I was twelve years old I stole a yo-yo from the corner store. And then when my best friend Annabelle was accused of doing it, I didn't fess up.

That's pretty mean.

Isn't it? I get hot in the face just thinking about it.

It doesn't sound like you.

I know! But it just goes to show. You can't predict. Who knows what I'm capable of? Now it's your turn.

I really don't want to do this.

I see you are going to require a lot of patience. All right, I'll do another one. When I was twenty-one I went through this weird period when I became afraid of everything. It was just a kind of general fear. I wouldn't go anywhere. I had to quit my job. I had to move back into my parents' house.

How did it end?

One day I just forced myself to get dressed and walk

to the store where I had worked. I was shaking the whole time. I threw up in the bushes along the way. But I went in and asked for my job back and got it. Going out the next day was a little easier. And slowly it went away. Sometimes it feels like it never happened. But I know that deep down I'm afraid it'll come back.

It must have been awful.

Does it worry you?

I don't know, I just found out about it. I don't think so. Not too much, anyway.

Good. You see, that's the benefit of telling a secret. You feel relief afterwards.

I'm just amazed how easy it is for you to tell me these things.

I don't find it easy! But at least I won't have to tell you later.

Well, thank you, I think.

Would you take my hand please?

With pleasure.

Thank you. So now you have to go ahead and tell me a secret. You can't possibly refuse now.

I'm starting to like this tree.

You're changing the subject.

I can't. I'm not like you. I'm sorry. Hey, what are you doing?

Getting up.

Don't!

What's the point? Anyway, you didn't want to lie here. I made you.

All right. Lie down again and I'll tell a secret.

I'm not going to force you.

I'm doing it of my own free will.

Good.

I don't really have to think about it. Here's my secret.
I have, in a shoebox at the back of my closet, a letter.
A stack of letters, actually.

Who are they from?

Somebody I knew years ago.

Who you were involved with?

Yes.

Written after it was over?

Yes.

I see.

You just let go of my hand. You're upset.

I did? I didn't realize. But I'm sorry I started this.

We can stop.

No we can't. What do the letters say?

I've never opened them.

And you've kept them all this time? That seems worse
somehow.

I think you're forgetting that I didn't even know you then.

As if that makes a difference.

So now *you're* getting up?

I can't lie here anymore. I can't — oh, I don't know.
No, I won't get up.

I knew this secret-sharing idea of yours was going to
end badly. Let's find a restaurant. Let's have some nice
hot soup.

There's only one thing to do. You have to open those letters.

Are you serious?

I'm completely serious. I'm going to come over and sit in your armchair and you're going to sit on the sofa and open those letters and read them. Just to yourself, I don't need to hear them. I just want to be there.

Is that really a good idea?

I don't think we're going to get anywhere if you don't. At least I can't.

All right, yes.

I'm going to calm down now. I'm taking a breath. I am. And I'm going to take one last moment to look at the most beautiful tree in the world, living or dead.

Will you at least give me your hand again?

Look! It's starting to snow.

BLOODY TUESDAY

THIS HERE'S MY TOWN. IT AIN'T BIG, BUT IT'S GOT good people and they need protectin'. We got a Main Street with a bank and a saloon and a hotel and an ice cream parlour. We got church-goin' families livin' here. Also hoors who live above the saloon. Hoors will sit on your lap and play with your tie if you give them money. They're sad but nice.

Around the town it's all farmin' and ranchin' but mostly ranchin'. On some days a whole herd will come down Main Street with the cowboys movin' them dogies along. Also there's Indians livin' up in the hills. Most people are afraid of 'em but not me. My best friend's a Moopawk Indian.

Now usually we got a peaceful town. But on a Saturday night it can get a little rambunctious. That's on account of the cowboys comin' in from the ranches to drink too much rotgut and ask the hoors to sit on their laps and play with their ties. Sometimes they break a chair for fun or accuse one another of cheatin' at cards or pour a drink on somebody's head or pinch a hoor too hard. Bein' the sheriff, I got to step in. Most of the time it doesn't take much, just a good hard look that says, *Don't you mess with me.* Other times I tap my fingers on my holster. Around here my reputation for bein' a quick draw is known to everybody. I ain't never been beat—that ain't a brag, just a fact. I tap my gun and the cowboy says, "Pardon me, Sheriff," and stops whatever he's doin'. Works like a charm.

A sheriff can't have a lot of friends, not when you might be arrestin' people. I got just two. One is Anabelle who is a hoor. Anabelle lets me sit on her lap and plays with my tie and I don't have to give her no two bits for it. And then there's Little Feather. That's my Moopawk Indian friend. Most of the time he's doin' Indian things, huntin' buffalo or sittin' on his horse in front of a sunset or whoopin' around a fire. He's got a sixth sense for knowin' when I might need his help, and then he shows up, quiet as a shadow. He don't carry no gun. He uses a tomahawk instead because it don't make no noise.

So on this particular Tuesday I'm walkin' along the wooden boardwalk that runs on either side of Main Street, just keepin' an eye on things. I'm sayin' howdy to the women in their big hats and pattin' the little ones on the head because they all idolize me. And then suddenly I hear a whole commotion goin' on inside the bank. A window breaks, throwin' glass onto the street, and some guns go off. A second later four men carryin' heavy sacks with dollar signs on 'em come out. They don't run off, though. Instead, they go into the saloon.

I decide to check on the bank. As soon as I go through the door I see the bank manager lying on the floor with both his eyes missin' cause they been shot right out. Also his hands cut off. I walk to the counter and look behind to see Miss Jennifer, the teller, lying on the floor with a big hole in her chest. Miss Jennifer wasn't a looker but still you don't like to see that happen to someone.

I go out again. My horse Daisy is tied up. I pat her side and whisper, "Got ourselves a spec o' trouble, old girl." Then I head over to the saloon.

When I go through the swingin' doors I notice how quiet it is inside. The four men who came out of the bank are sittin' at a table with a bottle of whiskey, playin' cards. Each of 'em has a big sack by his chair and a hoor in his lap playin' with his tie. The biggest fellow, huge as an ox, has Anabelle on his lap. Anabelle gives me a quick look, as if to say, *Don't mess with this one, Sheriff.*

As if I would back down from my duty.

I walk up to the bar. Behind it the Jew barkeep is shakin' in his boots. "Pour me one, will ya?" I say and when he does I drink it down in one gulp, doesn't sting or anythin'. I say, "Why don't you play that banjo of yers?"

"Vat gut iz muzic now, Sheriff?" he asks.

"Well, I'd appreciate it all the same." I give him a knowin' look.

"Okay," says the barkeep. He takes his ol' banjo from

behind the bar and puts it on his knee and starts to play "Darlin' Clementine," my favourite song. I nod and walk to the table where those four bank-robbin' sons of bitches is sittin'.

"Sorry, fellas," I say, "but you chose the wrong bank to rob."

One of the fellas pushes the hoor off his lap and gets up. He's got a pair of six-shooters low on his hips. The few people inside the saloon move away as far as they can.

"You could do yerself a favour and give yerself up," I say.

"And you can go play with yer toys," he says.

I don't like anyone mentionin' my toys in a disparagin' manner. But I know not to lose my cool. "Go ahead," I say. "You draw first."

He squints an eye at me and a split second later goes for his guns. He's fast but not fast enough and quicker 'en you can spit I shoot off his right ear. A little fountain o' blood spurts up. He gets a shot off but I duck, and even as I hear the mirror shatter I pull the trigger, rippin' off his nose. Black gunk comes out. "This is for Miss Jennifer," I say, gettin' him in the forehead. He wobbles a moment and collapses in a disgustin' heap.

"Hey, you can't do that," says the second robber. He too dumps his hoor and gets up. Only he's got a bullwhip hidden beside him and uses it to lash the gun right out of my hand. It clatters along the floor.

"Let's be reasonable," I say, taking a step toward him. "We can settle this peaceably if you just give yerself up."

"You is unarmed, Sheriff. I'm going to blow your law-abidin' brains out."

He draws his own gun but takes his time like he's relishin' the moment. Just gives me time to draw a knife from my boot and slash his fingers to the bone. Which of course means the gun drops to the floor. He's holding up his hand and looking at it with a dumb expression, and I stick my knife into his gut up to the hilt. I should have aimed higher because smelly poo comes out of him.

"Ew," says Anabelle, putting her French-perfumed handkerchief to her nose.

"Anabelle," I say, "come away from that ugly mountain."

"Who you callin' ugly?" the third robber says and lunges forward, putting his big hands around my neck. He knocks my hat off, too, but luckily it's on a string and just hangs behind. Now he's chokin' me with all his might, and I start to see stars and the faces of my ma and pa when I spy Little Feather creepin' under a table. He jumps up and plants his tomahawk into the ugly mountain's head. It goes in so deep that Little Feather has to push his moccasin against the guy's ugly back to pull it out again. Then he uses it to cut off the robber's head, which rolls across the floor with the tongue lolling out.

I pick up my gun and point it at the fourth robber. He puts up his hands. "I surrender," he says.

"Smart of you," I say. I turn to Little Feather. "Thank you, my redskin friend."

"Your life is always worth more than mine," says Little Feather.

"Let me buy you a drink."

"I don't touch firewater. Now I will go and dance in a circle."

Little Feather runs out of the saloon.

"You saved us," says Anabelle. "Come sit in my lap so I can play with your tie, no charge."

"In a minute," I say. "I still got some rough justice to do."

That's when I take the fourth robber outside, put him up on Daisy, and tie his hands behind his back. There's a half-dead tree in front of the ice cream parlour. I put a noose around his neck, fix the end to a high branch, and yank Daisy out from under him. As I'm not bloodthirsty by nature I do not enjoy the sound of the robber squealing like a drowning pig until his air runs out.

Then I head back into the saloon. It's a good day's work for a sheriff and I figure I deserve another drink. Besides, Anabelle is waitin' for me.

ROSIE

EVERYBODY LIKED HER. SHE WORKED IN THE FASHION-dress department, after being promoted from women's shoes, and was known to have one of the best sales records in the store. It wasn't just that she knew the products—it was how she could look at a woman and size up not just what was right for her according to size, age, etc., but also how she wanted to be seen. Customers were loyal to Rosie and asked when she'd next be on the floor. They would come in and find that she had put something aside, a dress "that must have been made just for you."

Everybody liked her, but she was my best friend. At least that's the way I thought about her. I was stuck in children's toys, arranging the boxes of games, the plush animals and Barbie dolls, the cowboy outfits and plastic guns. The toy department was just across from dresses so that mothers could leave their children for a moment—which meant leaving them with me. I felt like I'd never get out of that department. Then one day Rosie asked if I wanted to take my lunch break with her, and we went to Lander's Cafeteria next door where she listened to all my complaints. "Honey," she said, "it's okay to find the kids annoying but it's not okay to show it. You have to flatter the parents and make them feel good about their brats." She told me a lot more that made sense and as I followed her advice my sales went up. The floor manager, Mr. Constantine, became nicer to me. I could see myself getting promoted to small appliances or even lingerie.

We started to take all our lunches together and to spend time on our days off, too, going to a matinee, double-dating at a restaurant with dancing (she always cared more about the dancing than about the man whose arm she was on). She would come over to my apartment and we'd turn on the radio and do each other's nails. I must have told her my entire life story, especially my failed romances and near-engagements. "Don't you worry," she always said. "You're a catch. None of those louts was good enough for you, but like the song says, you'll know when the right one comes along. Then I'll dance all night at your wedding."

"Dance? You'll be my maid of honour."

"Now you know that's not going to happen."

"Because you're Negro or Chinese or something? You think I care?"

"Actually, I'm a whole mix of things. I call myself *Polynesian*. But it will matter to your family and you don't need that kind of headache, not on your wedding day."

I looked at her with so much fondness. "Let me find the guy first and then we can argue about it."

At Christmas time my two flatmates and I decided to have a party. Of course there was a store party but it was so phony, the bosses pretending to be our friends or drinking too much and getting fresh. At our party there were only people we really liked. We had a tree that touched the ceiling, lots of food and booze, a stack of Benny Goodman records. We packed the place. It was noisy and fun and, as the night went on, a little wild.

My brother was one of the guests. He was two years younger than me and hadn't yet found his feet. He never stuck at one job for long and had to live with our parents outside the city. He'd had a girlfriend I didn't like very much and wouldn't you know she broke his poor heart. As far as I knew he hadn't gone out since, so my ears pricked up when he whispered to me, "Who is *that?*" He was looking across the room.

"I've told you about Rosie."

"About a million times. But I never saw her before. Come and introduce me."

My brother looked like someone had blown fairy dust into his eyes. I took him over and of course Rosie was gracious and charming. I left them to check on the food and when I looked back I saw them still talking. The party went late but always when I looked they were together. Already I was fantasizing about Rosie as my sister-in-law. And then, some time after one in the morning, I saw her walk quickly to the door and leave the apartment with her coat.

"Did you make a pass at her?" I hissed at my brother.

"All I did was ask her for dinner. She said no so I asked if she had a boyfriend but she doesn't. I just pressed a little, that's all. She said I was being mean and then she stormed out. I don't know what the problem was."

The rest of the party was a washout for me. On Monday I saw Rosie at work. When we sat down for lunch she looked sad. She said my brother was sweet and reminded her of me but that going out with him would only end up with one or both of them getting hurt. I tried to convince her that she was wrong but she refused to listen. After that there was a strain in our friendship. Some days Rosie said she couldn't have lunch with me. We skipped two whole weekends seeing each other.

It was about then that I noticed that Mr. Constantine was showing a lot of attention to Rosie. He would stop in the dress department and ask her about this and that. He'd make a joke and Rosie would pretend to laugh. Mr. Constantine was known to bother the salesgirls; I had been warned from the start not to be caught alone in a room with him. Was that why Rosie didn't want to see my brother? Could she possibly be hoping to land Mr. Constantine? But a man like him wanted only one thing. Besides, I could see she didn't like him and that whenever he came by she looked nervous and busied herself straightening the racks. Once I even saw her shaking her head while he pressed a hand to her shoulder.

I wanted to help Rosie but didn't know how. If I com-plained, the management would never believe a salesgirl over Mr. Constantine. The only way to get free was to quit, and then there was the risk that he wouldn't give her a letter of reference. All she could do was endure.

One night my brother came over. He surprised me by saying that Rosie had relented and that they'd had dinner at Chez Michel. Not just once but several times. He said they had taken evening walks and held hands and once had stopped under a tree and kissed. He said that kiss was the greatest moment of his life, that it *transported* him — that was his word.

I was stunned that Rosie hadn't said anything to me. The next day I insisted that she come for lunch with me and I confronted her. She started crying. "I don't want him to get hurt. I don't want either of us to." I tried to tell her it didn't have to end that way but she said that I didn't know what the world was really like. I don't know if talk-ing to me caused her to act, but the next time she saw my brother she told him that it was over and that she could never see him again. That night my brother telephoned and I could hear him alternate between anger and tears.

No matter what, I decided, I would talk to Rosie again. When I got to work in the morning she was already put-ting new merchandise on display and she avoided look-ing at me. I didn't care — I would ambush her at lunch if necessary, would tell her that what she was doing wasn't fair to her or my brother. I found it very hard to concen-trate but business was slow anyway and a lot of the time

I was alone in my department. Needing a drink from the water fountain, I walked across the floor, all the while looking in vain for Rosie. Then I saw Mr. Constantine walk swiftly away from the staff area. Something made me hurry back there and, hearing a sound like a whimper, I pulled aside the curtain to the small employee changing area and saw Rosie. She was crying and her makeup had run but what shocked me was seeing her dress on the floor. Rosie stood there in her bra and panties and I could see that she was a man. A man dressed as a woman. I turned around and walked straight back to my own department.

Rosie didn't return to dresses. In fact, I never saw her—or him—again. The next day all the girls were talking about how she had suddenly quit, or been fired, nobody could agree. I ought to have tried to phone her right away but I didn't. I waited almost a week and when I finally dialled her number there was no answer.

I had lost my best friend. It almost felt as if she had died and I was in mourning. It wasn't my intention to tell anyone the truth about Rosie, least of all my brother. But a couple of months later he was still brooding about her, refusing to see other women, insisting that there was no longer a possibility of happiness for him. He came over to my apartment and quickly downed two shots of bourbon. I knew that I had to shake him out of it, so I told him the truth. I told him that Rosie wasn't a woman but a man, with a man's parts and everything.

My brother stared into his glass. "Did you hear me?"

I demanded. "Did you hear what I actually said?"

"I love her," he said. "I'll never love anybody else."

He already knew. I put my arms around my brother and held him tight. And I thought that it was terrible, just terrible that we had lost her.

JEALOUSY

T HE NEWS THAT UNCLE JESS WAS GETTING MARRIED sure took us by surprise. Everyone had said that he was a perennial bachelor, which, as a kid, I didn't understand was shorthand for homosexual. Until then he'd survived by taking odd jobs here and there, helping somebody out or acting as a middleman for certain deals that involved a carload of cigarettes or radios that had somehow become "lost." He also borrowed money from just about everyone, never a large sum, and he would become offended if a person suggested he didn't intend to pay it back.

Nobody ever stayed mad at Uncle Jess; he was always forgiven and welcomed again. People liked to buy him a pint or a meal, or hand him a cigar. He was good company, always with a story that he swore was true, or else a series of jokes "not intended for the ladies" that he would proceed to tell in front of everyone. In his inner pocket he kept two or three funny postcards—a woman wearing only stockings riding a bicycle backwards, two kangaroos in a boxing ring. "That Jess, he's about good for nothing," people would say, but they'd always be smiling.

He was my mother's brother, the youngest of four and the only boy—which explained why he'd been so spoiled growing up. She was the next youngest and so the closest to him, the one he would go to when in trouble, standing at the door with his hat in his hands saying, "I've really done it this time, sis." It was also to us that he brought his new bride. No warning at all, he just showed up with a woman twelve years older and six inches taller on his arm, a horsey woman with a lot of makeup and a fur collar and jangly earrings. Over dinner we tried to follow the story of how they met—a disputed taxi cab, a cruise ship, several jazz musicians, and a cop—summed up by Jess as "a case of mistaken identity." When exactly had they gotten married, my mother wanted to know. Three days before, at city hall. She held out her hand to show off the ring he had picked out for her to buy.

Pauline Manning was her name, and she was a widow. He had already moved into her flat and a couple of weeks later used her money to buy a smoke shop. Really it wasn't much more than a newsstand with walls and a door but it had a fairly brisk trade. He talked about his pride at being a shop owner while Pauline looked at him with dovey eyes. He told me that any time I came by he had a stick of gum waiting. I thought the shop sounded great but my parents looked grim. I knew what they were thinking:

What would happen when the bloom was off the rose, when Pauline began to see Jess for what he was?

But she never did. Or she did but still loved him. "My good for nothing," she called Uncle Jess with affection, or else "my little man," even after he began to lose interest in the smoke shop and would close it up for hours at a time so that he could go for a drink, or to the track, or to the the hair salon where Pauline worked so he could surprise her with a handful of daisies pulled from somebody's garden. Quite possibly she never expected him to make a living and the smoke shop was just to keep him out of trouble.

Uncle Jess had always come to us for a meal once a week and didn't see any reason to end the tradition, so now we got Pauline, too. One night my mother asked point blank whether they intended to have children because, if so, time was surely running out. "Oh," Pauline said, "we're seriously thinking about a little one, aren't we, my little man?" and laughed her horsey laugh.

What they were thinking turned out to be Lucille. A tiny puppy, she fit in Uncle Jess's cupped hands. Of course I was thrilled when they brought her over, but my parents just shook their heads, realizing that my uncle had married a woman who was no more mature than he was. The dog was supposed to be Pauline's but it soon became clear that the puppy had attached itself to Uncle Jess. And since she worked most days at the hairdresser's, he was the one who looked after the dog.

He took Lucille everywhere. She slept by his feet when

he manned the smoke shop, and waited outside the saloon door when he went for a drink. Uncle Jess cooed to her: "Who's my goody girl, who's my sweetheart? How about a kiss, then?" He let the dog lick him on the mouth, which made my mother say she wanted to spit.

I think it was a full year before I began to detect something wrong, a dark little cloud over Pauline. She started making comments about how Jess spoiled Lucille with too many treats, about how he never talked to *her* so nicely. "Now, don't say that," Uncle Jess remonstrated. "You'll hurt Lucille's feelings."

"Jealous," my father said one night after they'd gone. "The woman is jealous of a dog."

"It's mad, I know, but I can't completely blame her," my mother said. "He does pay a lot of attention to that mutt."

"It's not a mutt," I butted in. "Uncle Jess says it's a purebred."

"Your uncle believes whatever he wants. And you're not supposed to be listening."

But nothing serious happened. Pauline worked, Uncle Jess strolled down the street with Lucille trotting at his heel, every so often the smoke shop opened for business. I grew to like my Aunt Pauline very much. She was clever and had a tart sense of humour. She wore dresses with big, bold patterns, the sort of thing my mother wouldn't be caught dead in, that she said were picked out specially for her by a saleslady at the department store. She asked me about my friends, my interests, and actually listened to the answers.

I didn't believe it at first when my mother and father started whispering about her being sick. She seemed strong as, well, a horse. But within six months Aunt Pauline was bedridden.

Now it was us that had to visit her. She said that her mother and sister had died just the same way and that she had always been fated for an early end. Uncle Jess was very attentive, fetching tea, making soup, brushing her hair. "I couldn't ask for a better husband, or even a better nurse," she said, a tear in her eye. The last weeks were agony and finally she had to go into the hospital, where she died even as Uncle Jess held her hand.

Aunt Pauline was buried in the cemetery beside her first husband, for they had bought the plot years before, but she had reserved the other side for Uncle Jess. "I don't mind. She was more than enough woman for two men," Jess said, laying flowers on the fresh earth. "I'll join her, but not too soon I hope."

His sadness was genuine; it was weeks before he smiled at our dinner table. But slowly Uncle Jess became his old self again. He opened the smoke shop for a couple of hours in the morning, and again as people were coming out of their offices. Otherwise he was telling stories at the saloon, or shooting pool, or standing on a street corner with other men, saying something under his breath about a woman crossing the road that would make them all laugh. He thought I was old enough now to look through the postcards in his pocket rather than just peeking at them: a naked man holding a baseball bat at an upward angle from his loins, a crowd of midgets in a rowboat.

If possible, he spoiled Lucille even more than before. During dinner he kept her on his lap. My mother reported that the dog now slept on the bed at night, her head on the pillow. It occurred to me that, although he had been fond of Aunt Pauline, Lucille was the love of his life.

One night he said to the dog, "What's a little man going to do?" and gave her a tidbit from his plate. Later when he left our house, I watched through the window as he walked up the sidewalk, Lucille keeping up beside him. At one point she got in front of him and he angrily shoved her away with his foot. Then he stopped, as if shocked at what he'd done, and picked her up. He held her in his arms and buried his face in her fur. That was when I realized I was wrong, that even Uncle Jess knew that a dog was just a dog.

WHO I'VE COME FOR

Boy enters. He looks at the audience and waves.

Boy: Hi, kids!

He burps. Children in the audience laugh.

Boy: Well, excuse me!

He tries to do a headstand and falls over. The kids guffaw.

Boy: Hey, don't laugh! I'm just kidding, it *is* a
       little funny. So who do you think will visit
       the library today? Would you like to see Old
       Macdonald, who can tell us more about his
       farm?

The children shout: "No, no!"

Boy: Oh dear. All right then, how about Miss
      Maple the flower lady?

The children boo.

Boy: Not her, either? You're not making things
      easy. I know! Let's have Slappy the Clown!
      He's so much fun...

The children boo louder, cry: "You stink!"

Boy: Now come on, kids. A puppet's got to make
      a living, you know. Don't be so unreasonable.
      Let's bring *somebody* out. I'm sure we'll have a
      swell time.

Boy walks to one side of the stage and peers past the curtain.

Boy: Hello? Anybody there? Yoo-hoo!

He looks into the wing on one side. Nothing happens.

(Voices behind the curtain:

    — Come on! Don't leave me hanging.
    — Fuck off.
    — Bring on the dog.
    — The dog's lost an ear.
    — Something else, then. Hurry up!)

Boy: Hello? Hello? Anyone there?

Death enters from the other side. He walks to centre stage, turns to the audience, and reaches out a hand. His skull rises from his body and hovers in the air. The children cheer. Hearing the reaction, Boy turns to the audience.

Boy: Hey, what's all the noise about? Did you see something?

Boy looks around but not in the direction of Death. He sneezes loudly. Death's two bony arms float up into the air. The kids stamp their feet.

Boy: Gee, all I did was sneeze.

Death brings his head and arms back to his body. He walks slowly over to Boy and taps on his shoulder. Boy turns around and jumps.

Boy: Goodness! Where did you come from?

(Voice behind the curtain:

— What did you bring that out for? Are you drunk?)

Death shrugs.

Boy: Funny, I don't think I recognize you. Are you from around here?

Death: Not exactly.

Boy: Did you just move in?

Death: Oh, I never stay anywhere long.

Boy: You're awfully tall.

Death: Not for my age.

Boy: You want to play hide and seek with me?

Death: It's too easy for me to hide. Besides, I don't like games.

Boy: Do you do any tricks? You know, like juggling or riding a unicycle.

Death: Nothing like that.

Boy: Give me a break here. I've got to entertain the kids somehow.

Death: I wouldn't know anything about that. I've got a job of my own.

Boy: What's that? I'm sure it isn't as a food tester by the look of you, eh, kids?

Death: I just do one thing. I do it over and over again, many times a day or night.

Boy: Gee, that sounds tiring. You still haven't told me what it is.

Death: I come for people.

Boy: You mean, to take them somewhere?

Death: That's right.

Boy looks at audience.

Boy: Now, kids, you must remember *never* to go with a stranger.

Death: That's very good advice. But you see, if it were my time to come for you then you would recognize me. You'd consider me a friend.

Boy: Well, I don't recognize you so that means you haven't come for me, right?

Death: You are correct.

Boy: I'm smart for my age.

Death: Below average.

Boy: So where were you before you came here?

Death: A hospital. I spend a lot of time in hospitals.

Boy: Oh, we don't like them, do we, kids?

Death: I had to take a very nice lady. Took her away from a man and a small dog sitting beside her.

Boy: A dog in a hospital! That's funny, isn't it, kids! Did the dog run around and grab all the bandages and knock a fat orderly down the stairs?

Death: No.

Boy: So who *are* you here for? Old Macdonald the farmer?

Death: Not for him.

Boy: How about Slappy the Clown? He's actually pretty annoying, isn't he, kids? You should take him.

Death: Slappy is going to live a very long time.

Boy: It must be Miss Maple the flower lady.

Death: She hasn't been feeling well for some time.

Boy: But I bet she'll be glad to be going, kids, won't she?

Death: Everyone is different. First, just recognizing me will be a bit of a shock. Then, in the excitement, she might remember all that's good about life, the things she usually takes for granted. She might get quite upset. She might cry.

Boy: A grown-up, cry? Isn't that a tickler, kids!

Death: But then she'll calm down. She'll take the measure of things and understand. She might even make a joke; some people do. *What took you so long? Sorry, I left my soul in my other suit.*

Boy: We kids won't get that. Well, does she know where you're taking her?

Death: Yes and no. It's considered one of the great mysteries of existence, what happens after. But really, it's not so hard to figure out, in a general sort of way.

Boy: Now you've really lost us.

Death chuckles and pats Boy on the head.

Death: But I haven't come for Miss Maple yet. She's going to hang on, feeling worse and worse, for weeks. It's cruel, but there's nothing I can do about it.

Boy: Then you've come for nothing. You must be pretty sore about that.

Death: No, not for nothing. I've come for someone.

Boy: Me?

Death: Well, not really you. The person who controls your strings. The person who took me from a life playing Shakespeare for *this*. Who sweet-talked me into being his partner and then treated me like a lowly assistant. Who made me play all the ridiculous secondary parts. The person who has been in control of every decision, every boring show, every penny, and who is finally going to get what he deserves.

Boy: That isn't funny. You wouldn't do anything that you'd later regret. I know you. I know you all too well. And these pathetic threats—*aah!*

(Sounds behind the curtain: scuffling, groans, smacks, cries.)

100

Both Death and Boy begin to swing wildly back and forth, their feet not touching the ground. They become tangled up in each other, a leg stuck out here, an arm there. They collapse in a heap as their control sticks fall on top of them.

The children scream.

The curtain jerks closed.

GREENLEES!

GREENLEES, THAT MOTHERFUCKER! THAT BACKSTAB-bing son of a bitch. Greenlees is dead.

I've spent so long resenting Greenlees—hating and blaming him, waiting for the day that I can show how little he means to me—that finding out about his death has unmoored me. That's the only word for it. I'm floating without a destination.

He's been dead for a month. How is it that I didn't hear about it sooner? I left town long ago, of course, had to pack my bags and take what few dollars I still had and leave with my tail between my legs. Leave with my own mother ashamed of me, my father refusing to acknowledge me, my brothers cursing me, my girl having become Greenlees's girl. That was twenty-two years ago. And in that time my mother died, my father went too, and my brothers all moved away.

But even though I left I kept up a mail subscription to

the town newspaper, where every small event was noted, where Greenlees's photograph appeared at the ribbon-cutting for his new factory, at the annual Farm and Home Exhibition where he stood smiling before a pyramid of Greenlees Boot Preserver, at the company picnic surrounded by happy children watching a puppet show. I cut the articles and photographs out and pasted them in an album. I needed to know everything. Otherwise how could I know what I had to surpass? And how could I judge, now, that my success was indeed bigger than his, my happiness greater? I would study the photograph of his face with its small eyes and thin moustache. I would use a magnifying glass to better see the wife who was usually just behind him, smiling shyly. Over the years she grew heavier (they both did), her hair lightened, and thick glasses appeared on her face.

How had she been deceived by Greenlees? Perhaps at first she might have been taken in by his easy charm and glib salesman's tongue, his wit and flattery. But later, as she got to know him, to see him as he really was, how could she love him and share his bed and bring his progeny into the world? Because there in the photographs, beside Greenlees putting a ribbon on a cow or shaking some politician's hand, were the children. First one, then another, until there were five in all, each a miniature Greenlees minus the moustache. They had been suckled by the woman who had once been my girl. Well, the whole picture made me sick.

Even if I can't prove it in a court of law (as I tried to

do), I will assert until my dying day that Greenlees stole his boot preserver recipe from me. That I myself learned it from a drunk Australian is no matter, for the exact proportions of beeswax to petroleum to herbal scents, and so on, were my own. Without resources, I had naively asked Greenlees to become my partner. And what did he do? He squeezed me out and then, when I vociferously complained, he turned the town's opinion against me. And so I left, or was hounded out, and for two years I scratched and scrambled to keep body and soul together, to save a few dollars. When I had enough I began to make my own boot preserver, boiling the ingredients on the burner in my rented room, finding an even better combination. I used a cheap kitchen spatula to fill the empty tins with the cooling paste. Then on weekends I went to the local market, to the dog track, and I stood with my product laid out on a soapbox. To everyone who passed by I extolled my boot preserver, how it would keep leather supple, protected, and waterproof. How it would restore the original lustre. Was it good for ladies' shoes? Of course! Could it be used on bags, purses, coats, saddles? Yes, it could!

Of course Greenlees didn't have to sell his product himself anymore. He had distributors, a sales force, advertising. The image of a smiling, mustachioed Greenlees holding up a sparkling tin of Greenlees Boot Preserver loomed from billboards across the country. As I stood behind my soapbox, people would say to me, "Is it as good as Greenlees?"

And yet I sold my tins — for ten cents less than

Greenlees's. One or two at first, then more. People came back. I became exhausted from cooking the stuff all night and then going to my place of labour in the morning, but never did I let up. In eight months I quit my job and rented a small warehouse space for a large double-boiler and a table for packaging. I had labels—yellow instead of green—printed with my own smiling face. One day a week I drove an old truck from shop to shop, restocking shelves. A hardware store with twelve branches placed a large order. Within two years my boot preserver could be found right beside Greenlees's. My billboards went up beside his. It was reported to me that shopkeepers now asked, "Which boot preserver do you want, Greenlees or Morgan?"

I became wealthy. I built a house in the French style, not unlike Greenlees's house (I had seen a photograph in the town newspaper). I did not marry, unable to let go of my feelings for the slip of a girl who had once been mine. Of course I dated beautiful women (the prerogative of a wealthy man) and was often photographed with them for the newspapers. Did Greenlees see these photographs? I certainly hoped so.

The marketplace, it turned out, had room for two boot preservers, and both Greenlees and Morgan thrived. But that wasn't enough for me, so I had my salesmen spread a rumour that Greenlees Boot Preserver was made with fat that came from the carcasses of stolen dogs. It was such a delectably awful idea that the rumour spread quickly and was even printed in the newspapers. Greenlees dismissed the rumour so casually that he offended some people and made others more suspicious. Before long a postcard began to circulate from hand to hand, a photograph of a forlorn-looking mutt with a sign around its neck: *Please don't make me into Greenlees*. I was sorry only that I couldn't take credit for it!

I knew that sales of Greenlees Boot Preserver began to fall because our own rose rapidly. Within three months sales went up almost sixty percent. Shops began taking Greenlees off the shelves. Billboards were defaced. A headline in the town newspaper announced that the Greenlees factory was laying off half its employees. Then another revealed the Greenlees family had put its house up for sale and was moving into a much more modest home. A few months later the company declared bankruptcy and shuttered its doors. Greenlees Boot Preserver was no more.

Now I owned the market. Greenlees had been an insect, a speck, and I had ground him under my heel. Now at last it was time to confront him face to face, to stand at his door and say, "Greenlees, you conniver and thief, you have finally gotten what you deserve." I got into my automobile and had my driver take me the 120 miles back to the town where I was born. I walked the streets, awash with poignant memories. Here I took my girl for a soda, there we went to the movies and afterwards had our first kiss. As I was standing there the wind blew an old newspaper against my legs. I picked it up and read the obituary for Greenlees.

How had I missed it? How had I not known that a month earlier Greenlees had dropped dead in his underwear? I had become so busy with the growth of my company that I had neglected to read the town newspaper. It was as if Greenlees had died deliberately, just to rob me of my moment!

I walked to the cemetery. It felt cold and desolate. I passed headstones and read the names of people I'd known in childhood—Gormley, Noonen, Cunningham. And there was Greenlees. I stood by the grave and imagined the man himself, wide faced, mustachioed, already starting to moulder in the ground.

Stumbling over the uneven terrain, I hurried back to the automobile. The driver headed to the other side of town, where the Greenlees had moved. I instructed him to stop in front of the house. It was small and almost shabby. The roof needed new shingles and the paint on the door was peeling. I did not move from the back seat. Surely *this* was the moment my life had been building to, not the humiliation of Greenlees after all but my own salvation. I took a deep breath, got out of the car, and walked the short path to the front door.

I knocked.

When there was no answer I knocked again. I heard footsteps and then slowly the door opened. And there she stood. My girl. Her youth was gone but her face still wore the same frank and honest expression.

I saw the uncertainty in her eyes, for I too had changed much. Then came the dawning recognition. *Yes*, I thought, *yes it's me, your first love.* She looked at me for a long moment, as if thinking of all the years gone by.

And then she closed the door.

I SPARE MYSELF NOTHING

Dearest Isabelle,

I am sorry that it has taken so long for me to write, but a series of circumstances—tragic, sorry, ridiculous, and finally triumphant—have delayed this letter all these months.

First I must ask, how are you? And how are your ma and pa, your five sisters? Will it be a good harvest? The weather here is so different that I cannot imagine how it is there. I hope your beloved Dora is well. Even now I can see you on your stool, dress hitched up past the top of your boots as you milk her. Ah, if only I could really see that, Isabelle!

I arrived here by train on the second of March. Although forewarned, I still found myself overwhelmed as I emerged from the busy station. The sea of humanity! The carts and wagons and bicycles and motorcars! The men striding purposely or standing shiftless, the women in their plumed hats coming out of shops, the efficient office girls hurrying along, the buildings rising four and five storeys—it was like a dream of the future. And that is when I looked down to see that my bags were gone. Yes, I was robbed within the first two minutes of my arrival.

All I had left was the suit I wore and three dollars in my pocket, as well as the address of where I could stay for cheap. I walked through the crowds (it felt like swimming) and got lost over and over but at last reached the street. It was crowded with carts full of goods and people haggling as if in some exotic bazaar. The man who answered the door took a dollar from me and then showed me to a room on the fourth floor that was already inhabited by three people. I was assigned the remaining corner, along with a mattress that smelled of mould and a soapbox to keep my things in.

Immediately I set out for my cousin's shoe store. As you know, my father had already wired Herman a considerable sum of money for him to take me on as a junior partner and salesman. But when I got there, the store was dark. I tried the door to find it locked. A notice pasted on the window stated that the business was closed permanently. My father's money was gone! A terrible feeling came over me. Tired, hungry, dizzy from the constant movement around me, I felt as helpless as a child. And it was then, Isabelle, that my shame began.

You have always said that I am naturally gullible, and that all someone has to do is look into my face to know it.

Well, that's just what happened. While I was standing there a woman stopped to ask why I was in such obvious distress. She was very well dressed and, I admit, also very pretty. In a moment I was blurting out my sorry tale. "You poor man," she said, touching my wrist with her gloved hand. Perhaps it was my condition, but I felt a thrill. She insisted that we get into a carriage at her expense. We rode uptown and soon were passing impressive brownstone houses facing a green park. She paid the driver and led me to a door, letting us in and introducing me to her papa, who sat in the elegant drawing room with a newspaper. The man rose and held out his hand, and when he heard my story he expressed shock and outrage but not surprise. He said that decent, honest men like myself were as scarce as hen's teeth in the city, and even implied that I was just the sort of fellow he was hoping his daughter would meet. I blushed with gratitude and pleasure. (You see, Isabelle, I spare myself nothing.)

The woman's name was Charity. She removed her gloves and hat, letting her tresses fall. She told her papa that I needed a good job, something that paid well, and that he must take care of me for her sake. "Yes, I see that," he said. "Do come with me, young man." Naturally I wondered what sort of work he could offer without knowing any of my skills, whether it would be in an office or involve some kind of labouring, but I followed him through the house and down a set of stairs. We came to an odd door, covered in ornately engraved brass. He knocked — it seemed a special rhythm — and the door was opened, by whom I could not see for it took a few moments for my eyes to adjust to the dim candlelight. There was the heady fragrance of roses. What I was slowly able to make out, Isabelle, I can hardly tell you. I saw bodies—naked bodies writhing together. Men and women, men and men, women and women, in couples and larger groups, like many-limbed, many-sexed animals. In the midst of one of these groupings I saw a young figure, hardly older than a child, male or female I couldn't tell, down on its knees before another. This youthful person turned up to me, the languid eyes found mine, and a most beautiful smile lit up the face. In that moment I knew the grin of the devil.

"Go," said Charity's papa, giving me a gentle push. "Give pleasure to whomever desires it. Take pleasure for yourself. In two hours' time I will pay you fifty dollars."

Fifty dollars! Whoever heard of such a sum for two hours' work? And yet I was not—I swear—tempted. Raising up my hand, I knocked the man down. Then I ran out the door and up the stairs. "A pity," Charity said from her chair in the drawing room, sounding not disturbed in the least. I dashed out onto the street and kept going.

I cannot tell you the terrible, guilt-ridden night I spent on that mattress. While I had not participated in the debauchery, I had certainly been tempted by Charity herself—tempted away from my upbringing, my intentions, and worst of all, from you. All that I could do to comfort myself was conjure memories from home. I remembered one afternoon when you and I picnicked in the orchard and you read me a poem. *The still, sad music of humanity.*

In the morning I rose quickly, determined to redeem myself. I began to walk the streets and soon found a job in a cafeteria, not even as a waiter but a dishwasher. Yet I was glad to get it and have been working there ever since, nine hours a day, six days a week, and saving as much money as I can.

Oh Isabelle, do you still have the photograph that I gave to you before my leaving, the one of me in my best clothes, gazing out into some gloriously imagined future? I ask you to take it in your hand and look at it now. I long ago sold the suit I wore that day, but I still have the tie pin you gave me as a parting gift. I imagine what is in your eyes as you look at my likeness: irony, suspicion, even revulsion—but also, I hope, compassion. You must know that I work only for the time when we will be united once more. I am still your man, if you will have me. I still see you skipping between the trees of the orchard, still hear the ripe pears falling to the ground. Do not despair; know that I have walked through the fire and come out the other side! And as for that woman, Charity (if that was even her name), I hardly think of her anymore.

I remain,
Your Lucas

CIVILIZATION

"SO WHAT DO YOU DO?" THE GUY ASKED, SIPPING THE head off his beer. We were standing at the bar. What a fucking question. Did I look like I was a scientist, maybe, or one of those male ballet dancers? I was wearing a goddamn suit and I was a half block from the stock exchange.

I drank down my whiskey and asked for another. "Grease monkey," I said.

"Ha ha, that's a good one. I got you pegged as one of those stockbrokers."

"Bingo."

"Truth is, I've dabbled a bit myself. Just penny stocks, mind you. But I got a good feel for it."

Did he now? Then he was better than me. Because right now I was knocking back another drink to forget the fact that I'd made a bad gamble this afternoon and lost thirty-eight thousand dollars. A little error that my boss would discover in the morning.

"So you want to guess what I do?" he asked, putting his calloused hands around that glass of beer like it was a woman's waist.

"Hmm. Let me see. You write the messages in greeting cards."

"Nah. I make chairs."

"Uh-huh."

"Actually, it's my father's business. But I'm taking it over. Slowly. Learning the ropes, so to speak. I was in college for a while."

"Found out they couldn't teach you anything you didn't already know?"

"Just didn't take to it. Too much talk."

"Go figure."

"My father'll be ready to retire in a couple of years. He started the business like thirty years ago. Pressback wooden chairs. Oak. We've got a few models but basically you're talking a high-back model and a café chair."

"You don't say. Next time I'm in Paris I'll look out for them."

"They just call them that, any restaurant or diner can use them. Actually, I made a delivery of six of them here, reason why I'm in the neighbourhood. We sell wholesale to furniture stores, too, although once in a while an individual comes into the workshop."

"Workshop, huh? Like elves making toys."

"There's still a lot of hand work, see. Not that we don't have table saws, lathes, sanders, what have you. But the final carving, getting the spindles to fit tight. Truth is people don't realize what an amazing creation a chair is."

"Me, for instance. Bartender, I'm switching to beer." I watched him pull it. Behind him were various things thumbtacked to the wall. Postcards, a newspaper article about police raiding a sex club, a sign that said *Charity begins at the bar.*

"That's right. People think of certain basic inventions. The wheel. The lever. The printing press. Sure, they're important, but if you ask me it's the chair that made civilization. Instead of humans squatting on their haunches, you've got them sitting upright, face to face, having a meal, talking, being sociable. You don't want nations to go to war? Put their leaders in a couple of chairs."

"That's just what we should have said in World War Two. 'Adolf, take a seat.'" I took a long draft of beer. How in the hell was I going to make back that money?

Geppetto here ignored me. "People think a chair is simple but boy are they wrong. It's not the number of parts. It's the tension. The stresses. What keeps the whole thing together, the legs from splaying out or collapsing, the back from splitting apart, or the thing just turning over. *Every part in proper relationship to the other.* I say that underlined. You know what a chair is like? A bridge. Think Golden Gate, think Brooklyn Bridge holding up all those cars and people. You know how much pressure a man like yourself exerts? What are you, a hundred and eighty pounds?"

"Don't flatter me."

"And yet if you sat in one of our chairs, which looks

almost delicate, you'd find it held you up just fine. And what's more, you'd be as cozy as anything."

"Would I?"

"Oh sure, that's the proportions. The height of the seat, the angle of the back. And then there's the seat itself. I mean, a wooden seat, how comfortable could that be? But you don't even need a pillow, the way we carve it. That's true even though some little old lady might use it right after you. You'd think there has to be a compromise—"

"Naturally."

"—and yet you don't feel any, that's what's so remarkable. I'll be honest with you, my friend, in my opinion the chair is one of the noblest of human accomplishments. I don't care if it's the throne of a king or a seat in some coal miner's kitchen."

"You're right there, *friend*," I said. "Because they've all got to hold up somebody's ass."

"Well—"

"They've got to absorb the odours from that end of the body. What the commoner calls a fart. Throne or kitchen chair, people are always going to release some wind."

"Yes, very funny, I get it."

"Blat, blat, blat, puff, puff, puff…"

"Now you don't have to—"

"*Bvvt!* That was a real one. And here comes another—"

He cold-cocked me. Caught me right in the jaw. I went down like a sack of bricks. I must have caught one ear on the bar as I went down, because when I came to it throbbed, along with my jaw and the back of my head where I'd hit the floor. I had a wet and dirty rag on my face.

The guy was gone. Ran out like a scared rabbit as soon as he slugged me, the bartender said. He helped me to the nearest table, where I sat down, and he brought over my beer and a bag of ice. I took a sip and felt my jaw move like a rusted trap. And then a thought came to me.

I stood up shakily so that I could see what I was on. Sure enough, it was one of the new chairs the guy had brought in. Still had a shine on the finish. I slumped down again, half sorry he wasn't here to appreciate the irony. I noticed how well it held me up, how naturally it accepted my large frame. Even the seat was as comfortable as he'd said. Well, well. That asshole was right. A chair really is something.

BAD RUFUS

EVERYONE SAID THAT RUFUS WAS THE SWEETEST MAN they had ever known. It was partly his demeanour, the slow shuffling walk and the slight tremor in his hands and the softness of his eyes—a gaze of pathos and understanding. His voice was higher than most men's and he was never known to speak in anger. Really, he didn't talk much and when he did it was to remark on the weather, always with astonishment, or to ask how your digestion was, a particular interest for him.

As a young man in the army Rufus had been a surgeon. He saw the terrible results of battle. He tried to save lives using the crudest medical surgery—mostly just sewing up or amputating. Asked about it, he would merely get a faraway look. After the war, he wanted nothing to do with medicine. He got a job at the train station as a teller, sitting on a stool behind the counter. He sold tickets to Staynmore and High Creek and Ravinsville. He knew where everyone in town went and when they were coming back. If somebody mentioned, say, Charles Merton, Rufus would say, "Took the ten-o-five to Pike's Creek with a return on Thursday." There never seemed to be anything on Rufus's mind but the weather, the workings of the bowels, and the townsfolk's train schedules.

He'd gotten married after the war. Margret Stuffhart—Peggy—was the oldest of seven daughters. She was a sturdy, hardworking woman who ran the house, kept a substantial kitchen garden, and raised pigs. But Peggy got some awful disease that made sores all over her body until she was only too glad to die. Rufus, they say, was never the same after that. He forgot to go to his job at the station and when he did show up he gave people the wrong tickets. The station manager finally had to fire him. At home, he let the kitchen garden go to seed. The pigs rooted under the pen and took off; it's said that their descendants, returned to a wild state, still live in the nearby woods. The chickens stayed around until the foxes got them. Rufus didn't seem to care about any of it.

It is an unfortunate truth that some seem born into this world only to take advantage of the weakness of others. Word spread that a harmless old man was living in the last house out of town, just waiting to be fleeced. Maybe he had money or old coins hidden in that haunted-looking house, maybe he owned stock certificates or priceless antiques. Before long strangers began to knock on his door—travelling salesmen, hoboes, evangelists of dubious sincerity.

These last were the worst. Having heard that Rufus was a widower, one self-proclaimed preacher stood at the door and said, "Brother, are you sure that you will be allowed to see your beloved in heaven?" This very idea, that Rufus might be forever parted from his Peggy, seemed to be what got him angry for the first time. Turned some switch among the cobwebs of his mind. He let the fellow in.

Much later, upon his arrest, a rumour began to circulate that Rufus had murdered people, starting with the preacher. This accusation was false. What Rufus did was give the fellow a frugal meal and then make a bed for him on the old divan. And when the fellow was asleep, Rufus used a sharpened scythe to shear off his nose. He did it quickly, and afterwards he kept the man tied to a press-back chair in the basement until the wound was pretty much healed. Then he took the preacher in his pony cart several miles down the road and let him go.

The preacher did not come back, nor report Rufus to anyone. Nor did the next man, a distributor of bibles, dictionaries, and also suggestive photographs of wayward children. Rufus cut the man's ear off with a paring knife. After that it was mostly ears but also pinkie fingers and any of the toes. It was later said that while Rufus did not kill a single person (it was a miracle, and a testament to his skill as a surgeon, that nobody died of infection), he quite possibly held the record for disfiguring people in this or any neighbouring county.

Although his victims did not bring the law upon him,

the signs of Rufus's late-blooming criminality were not hard to find. He left them all about the house — a ceramic bowl of ears looking rather like dried potato skins, a windowsill lined with toes that were mistaken by visitors for dead baby mice. He might never have been caught if a policeman hadn't knocked on his door one night, looking for a man who manufactured and hawked a product called Ferkin's Fierce Digestive Cure, whose contents had poisoned a dozen people. Rufus had been doubly offended by this man's preying on those with stomach ailments, and had cut out the man's all-too-articulate tongue. His recovery had been understandably slow; he was still in the cellar when the policeman arrived, and Rufus, tired of feeding the man liquids, had led the officer to him.

The trial made sensational headlines and the courtroom in the capital was packed, but since Rufus pleaded guilty the show was over in a few days. Despite an aggressive prosecution, which presented a good deal of physical evidence, Rufus received a sentence of only six years. I believe it was his gaze that softened the jury. He served without complaint and became the prison barber. Upon release, he could not return to his house, which had been burned down by vandals. Instead he stayed in the capital, taking a room in a boarding house. There he lived out the rest of his years in obscurity, his identity a secret to those few who had any small dealings with him. But after he died an obituary appeared in the newspaper of his hometown. "Rufus was one of those riddles of humanity," its author wrote, "who prove that even the simplest among us contain unknowable depths." It was a pretty turn of phrase, if one that showed its author to be perhaps too enamoured of his own words.

LOOK HERE

S HE USED TO FIND IT TRICKY TO GET THE FILM TAB on the roller, but now she could do it in the dark closet so as not to lose the first couple of frames. Her sister was shouting from downstairs but she didn't answer, only closed the back of the camera and hurried down.

"Josephine, dear," said her mother. "You need a coat. And look, one of your socks is falling down."

"She likes it that way," Eleanor said, holding the bowl of potato salad. "She thinks it makes her look *bohemian*."

Josephine stuck out her tongue. "I thought you didn't even want to go."

"Of course I don't want to go, what's that got to do with it?" her sister said. "Our *duty* is to go."

"And it's your duty to join the army, Eleanor," she said. "You'd make a good general."

"I would, actually, if they'd let me."

Their father poked his head in from the porch. "Have you got your camera, Jo?"

"When doesn't she? It's like a growth. A third eye."

"I can answer for myself."

"If you're actually listening for a change. You must be married to that thing. I don't think you've even looked at anything except through the peephole since you got it."

"It's a viewfinder."

"Stop, you two," said their mother. "Now get in the car. And Josephine, I want a nice portrait of your grandmother. Do you hear me? A person doesn't turn ninety-two every day."

"Mother, you know I'm not that kind of photographer."

"Close the door so we can drive without somebody falling out," her father said. "Now, Jo, exactly what kind of photographer are you? It's meant as a serious question. I'm interested."

"I'm an artistic photographer. I'm not interested in subject matter. I'm interested in light and shadow and angles and textures."

"So you're the kind of photographer that nobody likes," said Eleanor.

"Art isn't a popularity contest."

"God forbid you should even *try* to be popular."

"God forbid you shouldn't."

"Watch your language, the two of you," their mother said. "And please don't argue."

"Are we arguing?" Josephine shrugged, holding up the camera to blow on the lens.

"I do like your photographs," her mother went on. "I don't always know what they mean but I like them. Still, I want a good picture of Grandma. Make sure you get her smiling. And remember how deaf she is now."

Eleanor began talking about the school dance committee. Josephine only half listened. She was thinking of the last batch of pictures that had come back from the Kodak company, their lack of contrast. She needed to develop her own prints so she could alter the exposures, dodge the light areas the way she'd read about. But even if she convinced her parents to let her use the bathroom for an hour or two at a time, how could she pay for the equipment?

The driveway was parked up and her father had to pull up against the ditch behind Uncle Reynold's truck. Eleanor held the bowl on her head as she marched to the door, their mother telling her to be careful. Josephine lagged behind, turning back to peer at the car through the viewfinder. Another step and her own shadow fell over the reflecting shine of the bumper. Mildly interesting but not worth wasting film.

"We hope you've left us something to eat," called out her father as they piled in. Greetings were shouted over the general din. Wanting to be done with her obligation, Josephine looked for her grandmother. But she wasn't in the living room or the dining room either. Josephine volunteered to take their coats upstairs. A gaggle of cousins squeezed past her. She went into her father's old room and dumped the coats on the bed. Turning, she saw her late grandfather's artificial leg propped up in the corner, still with a shoe on it. She squatted to get an upward angle and clicked the shutter.

She held the rail at the top of the stairs and looked down at the jostle of people below, but the view didn't please her. She moved halfway down and framed the tops of heads against the wall, clicked the shutter.

She went back down. Eleanor hurried up to whisper, "Did you see Tom? He's trying to grow a moustache. I laughed right in his face."

"I probably will, too. Have you seen Grandma?"

"Nope. I'm starving. Come eat with me?"

Her father was on the sofa with his brothers, a heaped-up plate in his lap. Josephine went to the table and grabbed a stick of celery, then a handful of homemade chips from a ceramic bowl. Instead of taking a plate, she continued to pick things up with her fingers. The table rattled and she looked under the cloth to see several of the young-est children hiding underneath. She lowered the camera and just as they covered their eyes with their hands she pressed the shutter.

She ate half a fried chicken leg and left the remain-der on a napkin. Moving around, she eavesdropped on conversations. Nobody mentioned her grandmother, as if they'd forgotten why they had come.

She aimed the lens at a glove left on a radiator.

She pointed it at Uncle Corey, asleep in a chair, sur-rounded by chattering people. She wanted to get him and just the torsos around him, and also convey the idea of voices and noise.

She went through the side door to the yard where kids ran about without coats on, holding out their arms, pretending to be airplanes.

Back inside, she heard Eleanor playing "Maple Leaf Rag" on the piano. She went down the hall, peering into rooms. The last was a small office that used to be her grandfather's. And there in his old armchair sat her grandmother with her hands in her lap.

"Grandma?"

The old woman stared at her without moving.

"Too many people for you, Grandma? I feel the same way." Josephine closed the door behind her. She looked at the shelf of almanacs, the needlepoint in its basket. "I like this room. I wish you could hear me better."

She crouched down beside her. "I have to take your picture, Grandma. You know why? Because it's your birthday. This is my camera. I saved and saved to buy it, isn't it a beauty? Let me just see here."

Her grandmother reached out and put her fingers with their swollen knuckles around Josephine's wrist. Patted her, then grasped her, hard.

"Ow, Grandma. That hurts."

She didn't ease up. Instead, she pulled the girl toward her. Whispered in her ear.

"Ghosts."

"Sorry?"

"That's what's in pictures. Ghosts."

She let go. And started to laugh wheezily, tilting back her head.

143

It began to get dark. People who had the longest drive left first. Their own goodbyes took so long that her sister pretended to faint. At last they were back in the car, the empty bowl in her mother's lap. Eleanor leaned on Josephine's shoulder and closed her eyes. Josephine thought of shaking her sister off but decided to leave her.

"Such a nice party," her mother said. "I think everyone really enjoyed it."

"Those ribs were tremendous."

"Josephine, did you get a good picture of Grandma?"

"What?"

"Don't say 'what,' say 'sorry' or 'pardon.' I asked if you took a good picture of Grandma."

"Old people can be very surprising," she said.

"That's true," said her father.

"Hmm, don't move," her sister muttered, her eyes still closed.

"You didn't answer the question, Josephine. Did you get a good picture of Grandma?"

She watched the dark trees passing the window. "Yes," she said. "I think so. I think I got an excellent picture." Leaves seemed to rise from the branches, and then she realized they were birds. "And I really need a darkroom."

INSPIRATION

S O, LET ME GET THIS STRAIGHT, IT WAS YOUR COUCH but also his. A shared couch.

First of all, it's a *sofa*. I hate the word *couch*. It's ugly. You want to be sly or hedge your bets, you *couch* your words. There's nothing sly about that sofa.

All right, a sofa. Belonging to the two of you.

Technically, yes. We got the sofa when we decided to share the apartment. It belonged to the person who lived there before us. We bought it from him.

For how much?

What does it matter, how much?

Out of interest.

Twenty bucks. We paid twenty.

And whose wallet did it come out of?

Well, his. But that's because he actually owed me sixty dollars. So he was paying the guy with my money.

And it stayed in the apartment for the whole time the two of you lived there?

It should take a vacation? Yes, the sofa stayed. Two years we were there. Well, twenty-two months. We got the place cheap because it had no hot water.

No hot water?

The owner didn't want to pay for hot water. He claimed to have some wacky belief about the healthfulness of bathing in cold water. Actually he was a skinflint.

What were you doing those twenty-two months?

Writing for television. Or trying to. For a show called *Out of Time*. You ever heard of it?

No, I haven't.

Doesn't surprise me, only lasted three seasons. It was basically a *Twilight Zone* except the idea was that every episode had to do with the concept of time.

So you were writing for it.

Like I said, trying to. Harry knew somebody on the show, an assistant to a producer. So we would write a script and give this guy a few bucks to show it to somebody.

How many scripts did you write together?

Let me think. Eight, maybe ten.

What were they about?

One was about a guy who gets into an elevator and when he comes out he realizes that for everybody else time is moving backwards. Only he can't talk to them because he's moving forwards.

That's a little hard to imagine.

Okay, maybe it was a little high concept. We had

another about a kid who, by shooting his toy gun, can make time stop for four seconds. That was a good one.

And did you sell any?

Not one. I'm sure Harry's friend showed them to somebody. The janitor, maybe. We were getting nowhere. I started thinking about trying to go a different route but by then Harry had met Harriet.

Harry and *Harriet*?

No kidding. She was a secretary at the network. She read some of our scripts and agreed to meet us to say why they were no good, like her opinion was worth anything. I couldn't go because of my evening job working the slicer at the deli. But Harry went and I guess the two of them fell hard for each other. I have nothing against that, I'm not the anti-Cupid.

But something happened.

Sure. Harry and Harriet went to city hall and got married. Then Harriet's dad, who's some advertising big shot, bought them a house in the suburbs. Before I can zip up my fly Harry's moving out. He takes all his stuff, he takes some of my records, he takes the sofa. I didn't care about the records but I needed that sofa.

Why would you need a sofa?

Everybody needs a sofa. You ever see a home without one?

But why did you need that particular sofa?

Because it was my writing sofa. I'd lie on it with a yellow pad and a pen and write. I got all my best ideas lying there. It was my inspiration, so to speak. I wrote whole scripts.

With Harry's help.

That's not the point. He never lay on it. He liked to pace around. He'd stand in the kitchenette and make bowls of potato salad using some old family recipe. He'd toss playing cards at the wall. But I didn't move. Harry would say, "Get on that damn sofa, we need to work." It was a very comfortable sofa and it had conformed to my particular frame. It *knew* me. What I'm saying is, it was my sofa.

So you didn't give Harry permission to take it?

Permission? Are you even listening? Harry moved out while I was visiting my folks. I came back and found a note on the counter. *Sorry, partner, gone to Shangri-La with my angel.* That was it. Not even his address—I had to get that from the mailman.

Did you ask for the sofa back?

What would have been the point? He took it without asking, didn't he? And he never paid me the rest of what he owed. I tried to get along without it. I would sit in a chair but my ass would get sore. I would lie on the bed and fall asleep. I couldn't write a thing. I *needed* that sofa.

So you went to get it.

You're damn right I did. I hired a company, Glenn Movers, and the guy, Glenn something, or maybe it was something Glenn, came with another guy. I had him drive us out to the house, took an hour to get there. I knew Harry wouldn't be home because he was working in his father-in-law's fancy office by this point, the sell-out. While the guys waited in the truck I walked up to

150

the door and broke the glass with a brick. They weren't too happy with the situation but I told them that I'd forgotten the key. And then they were suspicious when all I wanted was the sofa. But they took it. They picked it up and carried it outside. Actually, a sofa is not an easy object to carry. They had to tilt it sideways to get it out the front door. And the guy helping Glenn, not in good shape to begin with, was hungover. Unsteady on his feet. He almost dropped the sofa as they were hefting it up onto the truck. Then we drove back to the city and used the service elevator and put it back where it belonged.

And that was it? Without a word to Harry?

I left a note. Right where the sofa had been. I've got that by heart, too. *Sit on this, you heartless son of a bitch.* But I never heard from him. He didn't phone me. He didn't try to get it back.

And it was just the same?

Except for a wine stain on the arm. Still fit me like the proverbial glove. I picked up my pad and pen and flopped down. And you know what? Working with Harry had held me down. I wrote better than ever without him.

So you actually sold a script?

To that same show, *Out of Time.* About a woman who finds an amulet that transports her though time. One day she complains to her husband that he doesn't treat her like a queen and she finds herself transformed into Marie Antoinette waiting in her cell before her execution. It was the second-last episode before the show got canned. I bet you Harry watched it—he loved that show.

And what are you doing now, trying to write for other shows?

You better believe it. I've got a million ideas. I've got scripts coming out of my wazoo. And not just trying. I already sold one to a show called *Remember or Forget*. You heard of it? Every episode is about a memory. Yes, sir, everything's coming up roses.

And you don't miss Harry?

Okay, fine, once in a while I wish the big ape was around. But you'll see, he'll get tired of rubber-stamping orders or whatever he does. He'll come knocking. Not that I need him to write, that's crystal clear, but he was better at female characters, and he could add a nice, sentimental touch here and there. He'll come knocking and just maybe I'll let him in if he apologizes. And pays me back the forty bucks he still owes me. Then I'm getting back onto this sofa.

GRANGER

M Y SISTER THOUGHT HE WAS GOOD-LOOKING BUT
he wasn't, not if you really looked at him. Mostly
it was his eyes, there was something too intense about
them, too wary. It was like he thought you were laughing
at him even before he said anything. And he was always
smiling, showing the space in his front teeth. Most people
with a gap like that, they know to keep their lips together.

Dad called him a greaser because of the stuff he put in
his hair, but he didn't mean it—he liked Granger because
of his skill. Granger was a boat mechanic and could fix
any kind of inboard or outboard, steering systems, even
rigging on a sailboat. He worked in a shop at the marina
and had an agreement with his boss to buy the business
when the man retired.

Funny thing, he didn't care all that much for being on
water and had no desire to own a boat himself. Instead,
he had a motorcycle that he took Betsy for rides on. She

said it was exciting and she just wished Granger didn't make her wear a helmet, especially since he didn't wear one himself. She said it mussed up her hair.

He'd ride up on Saturday evening and Betsy would run out and climb on behind him. Then they'd roar off. I was only eleven and the idea of going on a date made me want to throw up. I'd heard all about what you were supposed to do. So anyway after they were gone I'd be stuck at home with Mom and Dad, and I couldn't help making some comment about Granger, how he just had a dishonest look, or how he acted like a know-it-all, which of course he couldn't be because he never even finished high school. One time my dad looked up and said, "I know it's hard to watch your sister grow up. It's hard for us, too." Which made me mad because it wasn't that at all, but I stopped talking about him because I knew they would just think it was sour grapes.

I didn't stop watching, though. I knew something would happen, that one night she'd come home crying that he was a pig and she never wanted to see him again. Or he'd get fired from his job for stealing or showing up drunk. Maybe he'd get arrested for something.

Meanwhile, whenever he came to the house he'd try to butter me up. "What's shaking, little sister?" he'd say. That's what he always called me, never my name. If I was on the porch reading, he'd sit down and ask what the book was, as if he'd ever read one in his life. Or if I was on the tire swing in the tree, he'd ask if I wanted a push. I always refused. He didn't even try very hard. He'd just say, "Suit yourself, little sister," and go find Betsy.

So one Saturday Granger came by in the afternoon. They were going to a dance in the evening and had decided to see the matinee at the movie house. I was on the porch (nobody else ever used it, why shouldn't I?) as they were coming out of the house and Granger turned and said, "Hey, little sister, why don't you come to the pictures with us?"

"Because she doesn't want to," Betsy said, really quick.

"What's on?" I asked, all innocent.

"Some outer space movie that everyone is yammering about," Granger said. "With one-eyed Martians or deadly blobs or something. You can explain it to me. You like that TV show I can never follow, the one about time travel."

"My sister prefers to stay home."

"Why, I'd just *love* to go," I said, getting up. "I'll just get some money from Dad."

"My treat, little sister. We can't all get on the bike, though, so we better hoof it."

And you think Betsy was happy about walking? But she just gave me a look and took Granger's arm. The sidewalk wasn't wide enough for three so I had to keep behind, but Granger tried to include me in the conversation. "So who's your favourite movie star?" he asked, dumb questions like that. But at least he wasn't embarrassed to be seen with me the way my sister was, especially when we got to the movie house because of course we knew half the people there. "Jeez, we're surrounded by kids," Betsy complained. "This is the last time I go to a matinee."

Granger bought our tickets and even got me a box of Milk Duds. I don't know how he knew I liked them. The show was crowded and we sat near the back with Granger in the middle. Every so often he'd whisper some question to me, like how could there be oxygen on the planet or why did the robot shut down at the crucial moment. There never was any logical reason but I liked the movie anyway. When it was over Betsy and I both had to go to the washroom so we got in line while Granger said he'd meet us outside.

Betsy said, "The next time Granger asks you to come with us, you better say no."

"And if I don't?"

"You'll be sorry, that's all."

"Hmm, I noticed that there's a war picture playing next week. I bet Granger likes a good war picture."

"Shut up."

"You shut up."

Betsy got a stall first. "Don't expect me to wait in here for you," she said. I got my turn at last, I was bursting, and when I came out again sure enough Betsy wasn't in the washroom or the lobby, so I went outside, but I didn't see her or Granger, either. They wouldn't dare leave me behind, would they? And then I noticed something going on, some commotion in the alley next to the movie house.

I followed the other people but at first I couldn't see anything and had to push my way through. Granger was in a fight with two guys — guys who were twice as big as him. He was still standing but I could tell he'd been hit a few times because he looked dazed and his nose was bloody and there was an ugly scrape on his forehead like he'd banged it on the wall or maybe the ground and had got up again. He had his fists up and was trying to dodge but the two guys were on either side, passing him back and forth, one smacking him in the shoulder, another clipping his ear. I must have shouted out his name because he turned his head and gave me that smile of his and then one of the big guys drilled a punch into his gut and he doubled over.

I felt as if the punch had hit me. I think I screamed but a hand grabbed me and I knew it was Betsy who began to drag me away. I tried to pull free but she got me around the waist and dragged me out of the crowd. She held my wrist and hustled me along the street, turning the corner as soon as she could. I kept telling her to stop, saying we had to go back, but she just kept yanking me along.

Only when we got closer to the house did she slow down and let go. I saw red marks where her fingers had pressed into me. "Why are they fighting?" I asked.

"They called him an Indian. A part-Indian."

"Is he?"

"Shut up!"

"Is he?"

"I don't know. You can't say anything about this to Mom and Dad. Do you understand?"

"I'm not an idiot."

"Hurry up."

We got home and it was a good thing our parents were

out because they would have seen something was wrong. Betsy locked herself in her room. When Mom and Dad came home she said that she didn't feel well. She took a bath and went to bed.

The motorcycle stayed parked in front of our house for three days and then, when I came back from school, it was gone. After that Granger never came around. He telephoned a few times, at least I think he did, but Betsy always hung up without speaking. A few weeks went by and I stopped thinking about him. Betsy began to date another guy, a boy she'd known in high school who now had some administration job with Howard Johnson. Nothing was wrong with him except that talking to him was like watching *Face the Nation*.

I got my first job, walking the neighbour's dog after school. One day I was out walking when I saw Granger coming down the street on his motorcycle. I'd imagined that he'd been permanently damaged, that he wouldn't look the same anymore, but in fact he looked just like before. My heart started beating fast.

He saw me, too, and slowed down. He didn't stop, though. He went slowly by, waving his hand and smiling so the gap in his teeth showed.

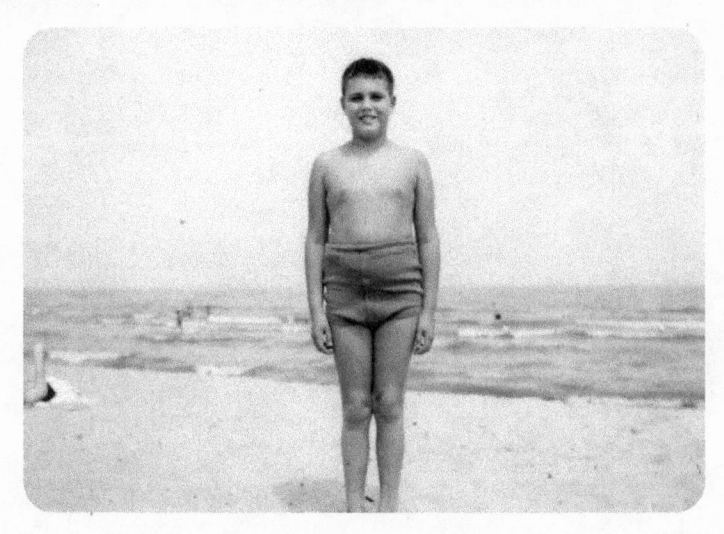

THAT'S MY BOY

THAT'S MY BOY

GORDON IS SHOUTING, "MOM, MOM, LOOK AT ME!" and all that he's doing is floating in the shallows like a little whale. Over and over I've encouraged him to make friends with some of the other kids on the beach, and he never disagrees with me, he always says, "Sure, Mom, in a minute, after I build this sandcastle, after I fill this moat, after I find enough of these shells to make a necklace." It's not because he doesn't want to, it's all the bad experiences he's had, kids calling him "Fatty," kids making fun of his naive questions, his excess enthusiasm, or just being mean because they need somebody to exclude. Kids can spot vulnerability the way mosquitoes smell blood. So how can I blame him for shying away?

But I worry. I worry so much about my boy. Sometimes I can't help imagining the life that awaits him. At the moment he's still getting invitations to a few birthday parties because the parents know us, but in another two or three years the kids will have more say and then he'll be staying home, all too aware that others are having fun without him. He'll say, "It's okay, Mom, I like staying home with you." He'll be sweet about it, uncomplaining, but what he'll feel I hate to think. Another few years and the kids will be going to movies on their own and riding their bikes to the park. And then they'll be teenagers getting their older siblings to buy them beer and hanging out at the quarry, and the girls and boys will notice each other in different ways. And all the time Gordon will be at his desk, doing homework, getting high marks that will make him seem even more worthy of scorn and dismissal. He'll go to the part-time job that he's found for himself, delivering newspapers or helping in one of the Saturday market stalls, and he'll save all his money because he doesn't have any friends to go out with for a float or a hamburger. Maybe he'll talk to himself once in a while just to hear his own voice. Or he'll become obsessed with some hobby like building miniature sailboats and he'll talk about it at every meal, how hard it is to match the colours of some historic schooner or get the thread to look like rigging. Then he'll graduate high school and decide he doesn't want to leave me and go to college, where he'll feel even more friendless and alone, so he'll get some local job, inspecting furnaces or maintaining public telephones, and he'll stick with it because everything in his life has told him he can't succeed or have ambitions, and he'll never meet someone who can love him for the sweet man he is, and he'll never know the joy and comfort of another warm being in his bed, and he won't become a father (he'd be such a wonderful father, I know it) and one year will pass like the next and out of boredom and depression he'll eat and gain more weight and I'll grow old and he'll drive me to the doctor for my appointments and look after me when I become ill and then I'll die and he'll have nobody to keep him company and absolutely nothing to live for.

And there he is, calling, "Mom! Bury me in sand, bury me in sand!"

And I call back, "In a minute, Gordon!"

God, I hate thinking about it. And maybe I'm wrong, maybe it won't happen that way. He might get lucky, or it might not be luck at all. Sure, it's pretty unlikely that he'll make friends in the next few years, the way it's going. But adults always like him. He might get an interesting part-time job, like with Mr. Hertz in the pharmacy. Whenever we go in there Mr. Hertz tells me what a smart boy Gordon is with all of his questions. Maybe Mr. Hertz will give him a job behind the soda machine. And Gordon will get interested in problems and why the pharmacist suggests one thing or another, or why the doctor told old Mr. So-and-So to take some pill or other. Gordon will do well in his science classes, as he always has, and his teachers might well encourage him to go on to university. After all, a lot of "weirdo" kids are science-minded, kids who march to their own drummer. So even without having made any friends he might want to go away, and given his good marks he'll get a scholarship to somewhere like

Columbia or Cornell or Harvard. In university there are lots of people like Gordon, people with different ideas, quirky, creative, smart people. He'll do well and other kids will accept him and like him because he's generous and willing to help others with their own complicated projects. And an idea that he got way back in Mr. Hertz's pharmacy will suddenly seem possible, and he'll apply to medical school and get in. In medical school it doesn't matter if you've got flat feet and can't catch a ball. The hours will be long but Gordon already has good work habits and likes to focus intensely on whatever he's doing. He probably won't be a surgeon—he's not very good with his hands—but he'll develop a specialty, like pediatrics, that allows him to deal with people. And while he's interning, some woman, a nurse maybe, will notice how gentle he is, how patient with people, and how much he's admired. She'll realize that he's awkward with women and doesn't know how to ask a person out, that she'll have to help him along, make it seem like his idea to ask her for dinner. Of course with such a big, needy heart, Gordon is going to fall for her. They'll have to wait until he finishes interning and gets a hospital appointment and maybe joins a practice, and then they'll come back here for the wedding, not a big wedding but lovely and tasteful. Then they'll buy a home and she'll work until the first baby and it'll be hard for him because of the hours and the demands on him, but every minute he's not working he'll be with his family—none of that country-club golfing nonsense for him. And I'll visit them often and when I'm starting to get frail Gordon and his wife will insist that I move in. They'll build a little suite off the kitchen with a private bath. And Gordon will be an honoured man in his profession, he'll have hundreds of grateful patients but will never lose his modesty, and his adoring wife will be at his side and his kids will take him as an example for their own lives. All of that might happen to my wonderful, sweet boy, and now he's standing and saying, "Mom, Mom, take my picture!" and I grab the camera and start walking over on the warm sand because I want to remember this moment, remember when he's all grown-up and I'm old and I know the kind of man he's become and the life he's made for himself, and I'll look at the picture and smile and say to myself, *That's my boy*.

COME BACK

COME BACK

W HO'S A GOOD BIRD, THEN? WHO'S MY SPECIAL
friend?

I am, I'm the good bird.

Yes, that's it, give me a kiss now. Ah, nice. It's a beautiful day, got to give you a little airing. Poor bird, cooped
up all morning while Florence had to go out. No wonder
you pulled apart my sweater.

Hee, hee.

And what did you do with my shell necklace? That
was a gift, you know. I'm sorry to have been out so long,
but Florence couldn't help it. Florence does have to work
sometimes. How else can I buy all that seed and all those
treats?

Bird wants a treat.

Now, didn't I give you one just a few minutes ago?

Bird wants a treat! Bird *wants* a treat!

All right, all right. Didn't you wake up on the wrong

side of the perch this morning. Now, how about we go for a little walk and maybe you can fly a bit. Wouldn't that be nice?

Nice, nice.

Good. Here we go. Look at the spring flowers coming up! They're so pretty. And the air smells like things coming alive. What is it, why are you cocking your head like that?

Bird hears. Bird hears others.

Yes, I hear them, too. Poor wild birds without a Florence to take care of them.

No Florence?

No Florence, no pull toys or pretty glass marbles or Mozart on the record player. No opening your beak like a baby bird for me to drop something yummy in.

Feed me, feed me!

Yes, that's just what you say.

I mean now! Feed me *now*!

Aren't you greedy this morning? All right, one more. Oh, what's wrong? Stop that, you can't fit inside my jacket.

Don't like, don't like!

I see now, it's that falcon circling overhead. And now he's perched at the very top of that tree. Don't worry, he won't come near you while you're with me. That falcon knows that Florence wouldn't let anything happen to you.

Why is bad bird?

That's nature, I suppose. What's the expression? Red in tooth and claw. It's ugly. But not with me. Not in your nice house, in your nice cage.

Cage small.

It takes up half the dining room! See, now that bad falcon is flying far away. That's right, you can stand as tall as you like. See how high the river is from the melted snow? It's really flowing.

Bird wants to fly.

Why don't you fly to that bush on the hill and back. That would be fun.

Bird wants to fly *high*.

That's not a good idea.

Bird wants to fly *far*.

We've had this conversation too many times. If you fly high something bad might happen. And if you fly far you might never find your way back.

Bird wild! Bird *wild*!

But that's just not true, silly. You're the tamest thing in the world. You like your food and central heating and the doctor when you don't feel well.

Doctor bad.

You didn't like the medicine but it made you better, didn't it? You're in a funny mood today, I suppose it's the spring weather. Let's go back, then. I can fill up your pool for a fun splash.

Bird wants out. Bird wants *up*. Bird wants, wants, wants...

My, oh my. Out with it, then. What do you want?

Bird wants other bird.

Well, haven't you matured? But you have me. I'm your Florence and you're my little man.

Bird not little man. Bird is *bird*. Bird need go bye-bye, see you later, alligator.

You can't just go off. That would be stupid. The falcons will get you, or the cats. And other birds will chase you and peck at you. Do you know that, do you even know that you're just a crow? You think you're the queen of birds, that you're a bloody peacock? The farmers are going to fire buckshot at you.

Bird go! Bird fly!

No, don't! Wait, wait! Come back here! Come back right now! You're a bad bird, a very bad bird. Do you think I'll wait for you? Do you think I'll be here in an hour or two or a day or a week? Because I won't. You can't do this to me. Oh, please come back, you selfish, horrible... Oh God, oh God...

Quawk.

What?

Bird come back.

You're really back?

Bird make joke.

Well, it wasn't funny. Not at all.

Bird think it a little funny.

I'm going to be sick.

Bird want to go home now.

Yes, let's go home. I need to sit down.

Bird want to watch *Rawhide*.

DAY OFF

IT WAS EXCITING, BEING A NURSE IN TRAINING, NOT exactly what I expected, but then how could it have been? The hours were long, ten- and twelve-hour days. And because we lived inside the hospital, in dormitory rooms, we never really left. All the talk was of work—which doctors were helpful and which to watch out for, who'd gotten blood and guts splashed over her, whether a particular patient died in agony or blessed quiet. And there were silly conversations about which doctor was the best looking, even though we weren't allowed to date them and would be fired if caught doing so. (Of course the doctors weren't fired.) But I never had time to think about such things, not when there was so much to learn and sometimes everything happening so fast and there was the need to react, react, react. The other half of it was just enduring. I was so tired those first weeks that I could barely drink my tea, and at bedtime I had to fight falling asleep with my uniform on, which was against the rules (there were so many rules). It got more bearable after the first few weeks, but it was never easy.

We got one day off, which I usually spent studying or else doing all the personal chores that had piled up—mending stockings, writing letters, buying my few necessities. The trainees whose families lived close by would go home for some good meals and the chance to be fussed over, but my family was too far and the best that I could do was take a walk in the city or sit down in a tea room with a book.

One of my patients was a cantankerous man with tuberculosis whose children had gone to Australia. But he had one visitor, a young nephew with no obligation to the man and who received no appreciation for his effort. The nephew's name was Edgar and he was an apprentice stone carver. His hope was to move back to the village where he was born and get work finishing the church that had been started there in 1740, a job that could keep him going for a lifetime.

Edgar clearly liked me. And he wasn't so bad looking, either, although his hands were rough as sandpaper and his hairline was already starting to recede. But I let him know, the first time I said good day to him outside the hospital, that I wasn't looking for a beau, that nurses weren't allowed to marry, and that it would be many years before I'd be interested in such matters. He looked disappointed but seemed to accept what I said. He told me that he had few friends in the city and would enjoy having someone to join him for a cup of tea or a walk.

Well, that was something I thought I would like as well, a friend who wasn't another nurse going on about work. I agreed to meet him at a tea room on my next day off.

We had a very pleasant time, talking about this and that. He told me about his parents and younger brothers and sisters, whom he clearly adored, and about the undramatic beauty of the country around his village. Talking to him was a holiday in itself. Our days off coincided so we made a habit of meeting, although when we encountered one another in the hospital we retained the formalities of near strangers.

One day over tea Edgar looked agitated, as if he had something on his mind. I got a little concerned that he might make some declaration, but what he finally asked was whether I might like to go for an outing in the country. His village was only two hours away by train and he'd like to show me where he came from. We could travel in the morning and have several hours to stretch our legs before enjoying a meal at his mother's table. Then we could catch the evening train back. He had already written to his mother and, he hastily added, had informed her that our relationship was strictly a friendship and that the family was not to get any ideas. At first I said absolutely not and acted as indignant as I felt, but Edgar seemed to expect that. We were adults, he said, and although we must be careful to observe proper decorum we were not living in the dark ages. And he was right, I decided, and finally told him yes. We made a plan to meet at the station the next Sunday morning.

I hadn't been on a train since my placement had begun and it felt a luxury just to sit and watch the passing buildings, then the factories and farms, and then the genuine country. It was a fall day, cool and a little misty, and as we walked away from the small station where the train had barely paused, the clean air was almost a shock to my lungs. We went down the road, climbed over a stile, and began walking across the fields. It was just as Edgar had described it, gentle rises and faded grass, the wildflowers gone until next spring. It felt so large and empty, just a crow overhead, landing surprisingly close to us and looking as if it might say something. We walked on, not talking as much as usual, but every so often I would glance at Edgar and see how happy he was to be in the landscape he knew so well.

The family cottage was just outside the village and when we arrived his mother was putting the meal on the table. She seemed almost too shy to look at me. His father shook my hand and grinned and asked me about my people. Edgar's brothers and sisters crowded about, excited by the presence of a stranger—a nurse, no less. When we sat down to eat they had all sorts of questions about the bloody wounds and amputations I had seen, while their mother kept telling them to hush. It was very lively and the delicious meal brought—how foolish—sudden tears to my eyes.

Afterwards Edgar's mother got the courage to ask me to look at one of the children who had something "itching him terrible." Of course I was glad to take a look and fortunately I had in my bag a tube of ointment that I could leave. It got late enough that Edgar's father had to take us in the cart to the station—take everyone, in fact, and a jolly group we were. We got to the platform just in time and skipped onto the train and then the whistle went and we moved on.

We waved goodbye and settled into seats in an empty carriage. I was tired from the fresh air and struggled to stay awake. I wondered what sort of day awaited me at the hospital tomorrow. Don't worry, Edgar said, he would rouse me when we got in. I smiled at him and leaned back and I couldn't help but let my eyes close.

YOU SEE ALL THAT

HOW LONG WAS THAT LAST STRETCH? FOUR HOURS? Closer to five.

I didn't think that driver would ever stop and give us a breather. What have we done, thirteen hours in all? And most of it without much scenery. At least we've got the water to look at here, and it's only another six hours or so before we get to your brother's. I have a pencil, want to play X's and O's on the placemat?

No.

Okay. What you going to order?

Pie à la mode.

Nice. I like that, *à la mode*. A lot of people think it means "with ice cream" but it doesn't. It means "in the style." See? Like what's in fashion. I might as well have the same. What kind of pie you going to have?

There's only one kind.

No, it says on the menu they've got blueberry, cherry,

and apple. I can see them on the counter under the domes.

I mean, as far as I'm concerned there's only one kind.

Ah, right. Apple. Am I correct? You know I am. King of pies. And coffee, got to have me some of that good ol' java. So what do you think of the others?

What others?

The other people on the bus. You know, who are having a break in here like us. What do you think of them?

I think nothing of them. I wouldn't even recognize one if I saw him tomorrow.

You kidding? You pulling my leg? Just goes to show how different people are. Me, I've noticed every one of them. I could describe them, tell you what they're wearing, who's a smoker. I've thought all about them—who they are and what they're doing on this bus. Oh yes, I've got my ideas.

I bet you do.

Sure. For example, that fellow in the old derby. Haven't seen a hat like that in years. Scratching himself like he's got some sort of skin ailment, putting on some cream. He works for a carny operation or sideshow, maybe. Keeps a greasy deck of cards in his pocket. He's probably got two weeks off and is going to see his grown-up daughter who hasn't spoken to him in years.

You see all that.

I can't swear to it but I do. I couldn't stop myself if I wanted to. Every face tells a story. How about that bunch of women travelling together? From some hick town for sure. Been friends for years. And now they're going to the funeral of one of them that got married and moved away, and although they're sad they can't help having a laugh, saying things that men don't even suspect they're capable of thinking. Having a good time, they are.

Is that so.

Then there's that man with the moustache. Thinks a lot of himself, he does. Not that he's got much money, you can tell by his suit. But he has other attributes. A scientific mind. Likes working out problems in his head, figuring the distance between two mountain peaks or how to get a ship in a bottle. He's convinced that one day he'll be known to all of us, like the guy who invented the electric blanket. Well, good luck to him.

If you're so smart then tell me something. Who do you think is carrying the most money?

Hmm, that's a good one. Let me see. Because it's not always obvious, no siree. For example, that lady in the silk dress. I mean, look at the work on it, must have cost a pretty penny. You might think she has a wad of dough in her handbag given her get-up. But you'd be wrong. Oh, she has ten or twelve bucks to get her through the trip. She spent her money on that dress because she wants to impress somebody. If she was rich she'd have good shoes on, too, not those old things. Maybe there's a job in the city she's hoping to get so she needs to make the right impression, show she can mingle with the hoity-toity.

All right, not her. But who, then?

Him. That old guy in the beat-up jacket and crumpled hat. He's got the most.

I can't see it myself.

Ha! Of course you can't—you don't have my eye. Sure, he's frugal. He doesn't waste his money. But look at that old leather case he's clutching in his lap. He hasn't let it go for one second, not even when he was dozing off on the bus. Maybe he's coming back from selling his farm to some Easterners or he's delivered a supply of moonshine. Could be he's borrowed the money to buy a prize breeding bull or a thresher. Wherever the money came from, it's in that case.

Well, well. You are good. I certainly underestimated you.

People have all my life. I'm used to it.

Now this is what we're going to do. No doubt he'll use the washroom before getting back on the bus. As soon as he gets up we'll follow him to the back.

Whatever for?

When he starts to close the washroom door you'll put your foot in to block it.

I'll put my foot in?

Then I'll elbow my way in and close the door on the two of us. You'll keep a watch on the outside while I rough him up a little, take the money, and convince him to keep his mouth shut. Then I'll come out and the two of us, we'll walk easy out of the diner. That's when we run. And we don't get on that bus, either.

What are you talking about? Put my foot in? Rough him up? I thought we were going to work for your brother building those houses.

Why work when you can take it for free?

Because it isn't ours. Because we didn't earn it. Because we're not crooks. Because he may be old but he's strong—he could knock you down and shout for the cops. We'd end up in prison.

That's why it's a good thing I've got this.

Where'd you get a knife?

Funny you didn't notice I had it on me, considering how observant you are.

Well, I'm not doing it. No thank you.

Yes, you are. Because if you don't I'm going to play X's and O's on your chest with this knife. Then I'm going to pull out your liver and make you eat it.

What is wrong with you?

Nothing except a perpetual lack of money. Okay, he's getting up. He's moving to the back. Go ahead of me. Go on.

All right, all right. But I still say—

Shut up.

This is coercion, you know. I'm being coerced.

If that makes you feel better. Move.

You don't need to point that into my back, I'm going.

Get the door!

I got it. Hey, mister! Sorry, this just isn't your lucky day. I just have to—*whoa*. That really isn't necessary. You can put that away. Don't point it at me. My friend here—ah, Jesus, where did he go? It's just a joke, that's all, you can take your finger off, no, don't, please—

THE OLD WORLD

W E WEREN'T ALLOWED TO GO OUT, ME AND KATHRY, and nobody would even tell us why except to say there was some kind of "disturbance" in the neighbourhood and it would be better not to. I hated that phrase, *better not to*—there was no way you could argue with it. It wasn't even late yet, just getting dark because it was October and the days were shorter, but the weather had turned nice, almost like the world was deciding it ought to be spring instead. I held my ball because I'd been hoping to get some kind of game going, soccer or one we just made up on the spot as we often did, but even though that wasn't going to happen, I still kept it as Kathry and I sat in the window seat and looked out into the street.

Every so often we'd see somebody, or maybe a couple of people, running along the sidewalk. Or a police car would go by with its siren on. Maybe they were chasing an escaped convict, just busted out of jail. Could have been a house — no, a whole block of houses — burning down. But nobody was telling us.

"Don't take up all the room," Kathry said, pushing her feet against mine.

"You're the one who's taking up the room."

"Well, I'm bigger than you, shrimp."

"I want to go outside."

"It isn't safe."

"Why isn't it?"

"I don't know, Raymond. Stop asking."

"But I'm bored."

"You think I'm not? We were going to skip rope."

"Now you have to play a game with me. X's and O's."

"That's the stupidest game in the world."

"Well, you have to do *something*. Tell me a joke."

"I don't know any."

"A story, then. Tell me a story about the place we come from. Before we moved to the city."

"Again? Aw, what do you want to hear about the old world for? You were just a baby. And I was only five, I hardly remember. You know that."

"Then make it up. I don't mind."

"You can't bother me for the rest of the night. A deal?"

"A deal. It was beautiful where we lived, right? That's what you said before."

"Uh-huh. On a farm. But not an ordinary farm. It was the greenest, richest, handsomest farm anyone ever saw. There were just fields and fields of things growing, tall as you now."

"What sort of things?"

"I don't know for sure."

"Please, Kathry."

"All right. There were fields of growing things. Beans and squash and tomatoes—for acres and acres, you never saw anything like it in your life. And the air smelled sweet on account of all the flowers growing around the house."

"Tell me about the house."

"It was a grand house, all white-painted clapboard, with a big veranda that went clear around and one of those swing chairs you could just sink into and swing in, back and forth, back and forth. And that's what we did, you a baby in a basket and me sitting with my legs dangling. And someone would bring me a glass of cold lemonade with tinkling ice in it."

"For me, too?"

"You were too young."

"Who would bring it? A servant?"

"We didn't want any servants around. Mama brought it. Then she gave you a kiss on the forehead and went back into the house because she was cooking up the most delicious dinner imaginable. And even though you were just a baby you could smell that good cooking coming from inside, and it made you smile."

"And there was a barn, if it was a farm, right?"

"Of course we had a barn. And horses in the barn, too. Work horses and ponies and even a racehorse."

"A racehorse! What was its name?"

"Hmm, let me think. Its name was...Ethiopia. And it

won every single race there was. And of course we had a beautiful carriage, for when Mama wanted to go into town. She'd shop for store-bought clothes, she didn't have to make anything, and we had something different to wear every day of the week. And she bought us candy, too, gumdrops and sours."

"And where was Papa?"

"Papa, well, Papa was in town, working in his office. He had a big desk, like the principal at school only it wasn't all plain and scratched up, it was fancy. He sat behind his desk and signed papers all day and people came to him to ask for favours and if he liked the person he would grant the favour and if he didn't like the person he would send him out again. Then when the day was over he would put on his fine coat and go down to the street and get on his own horse, which was big and white, and he would gallop home just for the fun of it."

"And people had to jump out of the way?"

"Yes, they did. And Papa would reach the house and give the horses their oats and he would come up the veranda stairs and pick me up and whirl me around. And then he'd pick you up and tickle you, and we'd go inside, and Mama would have the most splendid dinner all laid out for us. And it wouldn't just be us at the table, it would be Aunt Ellie and Aunt Del and our cousins Will and Jake and Roland and Grandma and Grandpa—all the people you can't remember and I can hardly remember—and we'd eat and drink and tell stories and joke and laugh. And then after we had our dessert we'd go outside where it was dark and I'd hold you and we'd all run around the big dark lawn chasing the fireflies that dipped and rose and the deer that was grazing on the distant hill would raise its head to look at us."

Kathry stopped talking.

"I wish we were there," I said. "Why did we move to the city?"

But she didn't answer. She never answered that question. Now she just looked out the window, where the wind was blowing a fedora along the sidewalk. All by itself it was moving, without even anybody chasing it.

MINUTES OF THE MEETING

Minutes of the Meeting of the Norton East Gentleman's Society for Scientific Inquiry, held in the private room of Hiram's Tavern.

SECRETARY: Attention, please. May we at least begin? If you will only sit down. The meeting is now officially commenced. I have tabled the minutes of last month's meeting. Will someone propose acceptance?

MR. HORNBY: I make the proposal.

MR. ASHLAND: I second.

SECRETARY: A show of hands? Minutes accepted. As some of you know, we were to have a presentation by Mr. Ostmann describing the latest trial of his leg-powered vertical-blade flying machine. However, as Mr. Ostmann is currently recovering in the Norton East Hospital—

MR. CROSSLEY: Two broken legs, ha!

MR. MOOREHOUSE: A toast to Ostmann, that idiot!

SECRETARY: Order, please. Let us not have this meeting descend into the anarchistic shouting match of last month. As for present business, we are fortunate to have a volunteer in Mr. Josiah Thorpe. Mr. Thorpe has offered to give us a sketch of his own current work.

MR. DIXON: Good on you, Thorpe!

SECRETARY: Kindly let me finish. Some of you may not be acquainted with Mr. Thorpe, the newest member of our society, the gentleman having only recently situated himself in our neighbourhood. Mr. Thorpe is a teacher at the Henshaw Upper School for Boys where he is responsible for teaching Greek, Latin, and all the natural sciences.

MR. CROSSLEY: *In vino veritas*, eh, Thorpe?

SECRETARY: Would someone make sure that Mr. Crossley is served no more libations. I myself am unfamiliar with the exact nature of Mr. Thorpe's investigations and look forward to these preliminary remarks. Let us now turn our attention, and the full power of our own rational minds, to the honourable member.

GENERAL (singing): *For he's a jolly good fellow,* etc.

MR. THORPE: Thank you for that that warm welcome. It is never easy to be the new pupil in class, so to speak, and I appreciate the manner in which the members of this society have made me feel welcome. Indeed, the main reason for my leaving Goldrich was the closed-mindedness of the society there.

MR. CROSSLEY: Shit on Goldrich!

MR. THORPE: Yes, well. Let me begin without further delay. In fact, I do not wish only to give a description of my work, but also to make a proposal. My area of particular interest is a conjoining of organic life speculation with developmental geography. Surely, gentleman, I am not the only man of inquiring spirit who has found flaws in the largely accepted notions of the workings of the sphere we inhabit. That is, earth. The perfect balance of oxygen, water, and other crucial elements that allow for not just life, but an amazing variety of creatures, many of which we have not yet discovered—all of this seems too amazing to be merely a result of accident or even of blind, amoral evolution.

MR. TURPER: You aren't a clergyman in disguise, are you, Thorpe?

MR. THORPE: It is true that I studied for the ministry as a young man. But my scientific cast of mind and my reading forced me to break from all religion. No, I do not make an argument for some all-powerful deity. Instead, what I offer is a new theory of life that has its origins in the very heart of our planet. That is, in the earth's core.

MR. PORLISS: Molten lava!

MR. SIMONS: Shifting plates!

MR. THORPE: Neither. I believe that the centre of the earth is quite hollow. Yes, hollow. And within this enormous space works a spherical mechanism, an engine as it were, created by minds far superior to ours.

GENERAL: (Much shouting.)

MR. THORPE: That's right. An engine created by the mind of a superior race—a race not of earth. To imagine this mechanism you may think of the inner workings of a gigantic and most complex pocket watch. I believe it is this engine, this clockwork as it were, that drives the living impulses of this planet.

MR. HORNBY: Is he mad?

MR. CLEMENZ: Give him a chance!

MR. CROSSLEY: I insist on another drink!

SECRETARY: Let Mr. Thorpe continue.

MR. THORPE: Thank you, Mr. Secretary. Next month I shall bring charts, diagrams, evidence, and conjectural drawings that I am sure will help to reduce your skepticism. For now I must plead with you to remember our great scientific ancestors whose own theories were rejected by their peers. Try to imagine this most extraordinary engine and the beings who operate it. What these creatures look like I cannot say for certain but I have concluded through reasoning and deduction that they must be small—say the size of a common squirrel. Also that they are extremely dexterous and likely have three or even four sets of hands.

MR. CROSSLEY: Shake hands with the intelligent squirrel!

MR. THORPE: If I might now get to the proposal. I wish to build a machine. A machine that will dig downward, much as we now dig tunnels under mountains for trains and the like. But it must be ten times more powerful. We shall dig straight downward until we reach the earth's core, an undertaking of three or four years. Only then can we make contact with the beings who are the true rulers of our planet. At the same time I propose that we convene a meeting of the world's greatest linguists—men from around the globe—to speculate on the structure and workings of their language so that we may begin at least a rudimentary discourse on our first encounter. Of course this will be a costly undertaking. Therefore I wish to establish a fund—

MR. SIMONS: Can't we just use shovels?

MR. CROSSLEY: Ask Hornby, his wife's family controls the linseed oil market!

MR. MOOREHOUSE: What if the earth is a giant ball and you let out all the air, eh? *Pssst!*

MR. THORPE: — a fund, I say, for the design and building of this digging machine. If we act in a bold and authoritative manner to convince the public, I believe we can raise the money quickly and get to work. As I say, I shall present all my findings next month, but if I could see by a preliminary show of hands —

MR. PORLISS: You're telling fairy tales, Thorpe, bedtime stories!

MR. FLEURY: What about my theory of intelligent fishes? Why haven't we funded that yet?

SECRETARY: Get off the table, Ashland! Crossley, do not throw that —

MR. DIXON: Mind control through magnetism!

MR. HORNBY: You're a thief. You've stolen my ideas!

MR. THORPE: Let … go … of … my … whiskers!

General chaos. Meeting dissolved without official closing.

THE TRAVELLER

I T TOOK ME A LONG TIME TO TRAIN MYSELF, OR RATHER not all of myself, but to separate my mind from my corporeal being, my body. That was the hardest part. But I had to learn if I wanted to survive.

Of course I had my piano lessons to give, and they helped me get through the day. The evening was what I dreaded most, and the time in the bedroom until he went to sleep. Only then would I feel the weight of his presence lessen, shift away from me, and my own tension ease. I wouldn't go to sleep right away; I'd lie for an hour or more, feeling the freedom of aloneness. Every time he shifted his bulk or snored the feeling would dart away like a frightened bird.

But when things got worse, merely lying there wasn't enough. It was as if I couldn't lift the weight of him off me, couldn't catch my breath. That was when the discipline began, the training, for I knew that I had to escape at least in my mind. I would lie very still and let all memory of the day slowly fade. It felt like snipping threads, one after another, hundreds of them. My hope was to simply turn off my life for a few hours, the way one might turn off a radio for silence. But something else happened. One night I got into a state of both concentration and ease, a state difficult to describe, and when the last thread gave way I felt myself float upwards—not my whole self, for my body remained (I could sense this) in bed, but my spirit or mind or soul or whatever one might call it. I rose up toward the plaster swirls in the ceiling and then stopped. I came down again and settled once more into my body.

Whatever had happened felt wonderful. It gave me hope. After that I waited impatiently for him to fall asleep so that I could try again. I couldn't do it the next night, but I succeeded the one after, and every night after that, only I got stuck in the same place, hovering above my physical self, unable to move any farther. Not all the threads, it seemed, had let go. And then came a night where I was particularly horrified and exhausted and despondent, when I felt as if I had nothing of myself left. It was very late when he finally fell asleep. I lay there feeling like a glass jar rolling on a table. The glass jar went over the edge and shattered—and in that moment all the threads let go.

The thing was, it didn't feel strange. It felt right and natural. The night was warm and the bedroom window was open. A slight breeze shifted the curtains. I floated out, over the small back garden and then the gardens of our neighbours. I saw a woman standing at an open window, smoking. I saw a man digging a hole. A cat on a roof tilted its head up as I passed over.

I didn't go far that first night because I was afraid of not being able to get back into my body to become my whole self again. I slipped through the window, hovered over my body (my eyes were closed, my mouth unemotional), and slipped back in. There was a slight tremor of the mattress that made him turn on his side. I was tired and went quickly to sleep but remembered as soon as my eyes opened in the morning. I couldn't wait for it to get dark again.

I went farther the next night, travelling over houses, the school, the park. Over town I saw the lights of the all-night diner, saw the one street light turn green and red and green. Behind the dark bandshell two forms lay on the grass in an embrace. I went lower and saw that the girl was one of my pupils, who came every Wednesday afternoon for her piano lesson while the boy sometimes waited outside to walk her home. I felt glad to see them.

These night travels continued for several months and made life bearable again. Over time I went farther, staying out almost all night. Below me I saw other towns, the escarpment, the lake, bonfires. But I always came back, always returned to my body before light. I still believed in duty.

And then for some reason he asked me to play the piano. He'd been commenting on the newspaper in his hands, telling me about neighbourhood disturbances and the deterioration of society. He put the paper down and asked if I would play something for him. He'd never had the slightest interest in music before except for the fees that I handed over. I wondered if my nightly excursions had changed me in some way, had given me a look or demeanour that roused his anxiety. Whatever the reason, he insisted I sit at the piano bench and play whatever happened to be open—Chopin, Brahms, Mozart, it was all the same to him. Perhaps he wanted to spoil music for me, to poison it as he had done with so much else. If so, he began to succeed, because I hated playing for him and that hatred began to seep into what I played. But I just couldn't lose what music gave me. That's when I decided to try and travel during the day.

But would it be possible to leave my body and yet continue to play? It required a tremendous mental effort even to try, but at last I rose up above myself at the piano. There was a slight hesitation, a sixteenth-note pause at most, before my hands continued. I saw that my body was working on pure muscle memory, playing the notes accurately but without the slightest feeling. He registered no change at all but merely stared sullenly into space. And so I left him there with the shell of me and went out into the world.

Travelling during the day meant light, meant there was so much to see. I found myself able to move over great distances. I saw ice floes. I saw beautiful cities. I discovered what a glorious place was the world.

And then I returned. Through the window, into

the parlour, to drop gently back into my seated form. Immediately the music came back to life. One day even he noticed, turning his head to look at me. I finished the étude, and he muttered, "Yes, well, that's enough," and got up to put his hand heavily on my shoulder. And at that moment I told myself that my courage would grow, would eventually encompass my whole self, and that one day I would float out the door, taking my body with me.

WHO'S SORRY NOW?

MONDAY

A maggot in my porridge this morning. I didn't see it until the thing was wiggling on my spoon. I dropped the spoon which splashed porridge on the inmate next to me and a second later the whole bench was on its feet. Then the guards came down on us, pulling out their nightsticks. A guy beside me got a stick in the ribs and another guard was about to come down hard over my lifted arms when the floor captain yelled, "Don't hurt him, he's in the band!"

I only had to scrub the showers, and when four o'clock came around I got called into rehearsal. We spent most of the hour working on "Sensation Rag." Of course we don't have a clarinet player so Siggins has to sub on sax. Three new fish are being transferred in tomorrow and we're hoping for a recruit. The warden's been trying to get us a clarinet or trombone player but we don't know yet. A tenor banjo would certainly bolster the rhythm section.

TUESDAY

Another attempted suicide today. Old geezer named Juarez tried to hang himself with a bedsheet when his cellmate was in the library. A guard cut him down and the doc came running. Juarez got taken by wagon to the hospital where he's alive but unconscious. Word is he'll never wake up. Same old thing.

No luck with the greeners, not a musician among them. One played B-league baseball and immediately got recruited by the team, the lucky bastards. At rehearsal we worked on "Tico-Tico," but ever since Cummings got early release it's become a dog's dinner. I hope we won't have to drop it.

WEDNESDAY

Today there was an unexpected visit from the governor so we got served hamburgers for lunch, a genuine treat. The big shots walked through the dining hall and then went to eat on white tablecloths while Reiter played violin. At rehearsal we asked him how it went. "I started with some Mozart but it was putting them to sleep. So I lit into 'Sally Goodin' and woke 'em up. Got their feet tapping. We might even get some new strings."

Everybody patted Reiter on the back and then we ran through "When the Saints Go Marching In." I'm bored to tears with that old chestnut but somebody always requests it.

Last night two inmates tried to escape in the back of the bread-delivery van. Brothers named Whitehead. Of course keeping brothers in the same cell block is against the rules and the governor is going to hear about it. The brothers pushed the driver out of the van and took off. They might have made it, at least for a while, if the one driving hadn't tried to avoid a cat. Said later it was just sitting in the middle of the road looking up. The van smashed into a mailbox and turned over. The other brother was killed almost instantly. So ended their sibling rivalry.

In rehearsal we made another hash of "Tico-Tico." I suggested we replace it with "Who's Sorry Now?" with me taking the lead. They were skeptical that a mandolin solo could be heard above the horns but we gave it a try and it went pretty well. Must say, I felt pretty chuffed.

Half the block was up all night with bad stomach runs. You could hear the groans up and down the block and the smell was enough to make you gag. Didn't get me, though. Some thought the culprit was the fish stew, others the butterscotch pudding. I traded my pudding for two cigarettes so I'm thinking that was it.

Rained all day. They still made us go out in the yard. We came back soaked and shivering. An hour later Taskins was sent to the infirmary with a high fever.

I got put on library duty. A mere seven months after

putting in the request. The library is in a space next to the laundry and the books get mouldy from the humidity. I went to pick up the cart and glimpsed two inmates, one with his pants around his ankles. Didn't see who it was, or whether it was by consent or force. Not my business.

Time getting short, we decided to run through most of the set at rehearsal. "Sensation Rag," "Jealous," "Bei Mir Bist du Schön," "Saints." It's official: "Who's Sorry Now?" is on the set list, which is pretty swell. But even I have to admit the highlight was "Tiger Rag." That tune is really starting to swing.

SATURDAY

Mail delivery today. Everyone waited in his cell, trying to look casual but actually tense as hell, not knowing if he was going to get a "Dear John" letter or find out that Mother has kicked the bucket. Me, I didn't expect to get anything and I wasn't disappointed. I just lay back on my bunk and read the book I took out of the library, *Call of the Wild*.

Full rehearsal tonight in preparation for tomorrow's evening concert. Then our "good" clothes were taken from us to be cleaned and pressed. After that we got an hour of extra leisure before lights out. I lay on my bunk with my eyes closed but couldn't stop playing my lead for "Who's Sorry Now?" over and over in my head. I could feel my fingers moving under the thin blanket.

Everyone in the band got a special breakfast — bacon, eggs, toast. We sat at a separate table and the other inmates shot daggers at us. Of course we gloated.

We were allowed to take our instruments into our cells. I gave my mandolin a good wipe-down. It's got a nice bowl, alternating rosewood and maple strips. Just holding it always makes me feel good.

Somebody called my name and I looked up to see a guard opening the cell door. "You, get up," he said.

"What did I do?" I asked.

"Come with me."

I walked in front of him. He didn't put cuffs on me, which meant it couldn't be too serious. Another guard joined us at the end of the block. "You got a smart lawyer," the new guard said.

"I don't have a lawyer."

"Then this is your lucky day."

The first guard unlocked a heavy door and then another. We took a staircase and walked a long corridor. We reached an office where the warden himself was at his desk looking through a file. He picked a paper bag off the floor and pushed it into my arms.

"That's your stuff," he said. "You have to change."

"Change?"

"You can't take prison property with you."

I looked in the bag and saw the clothes that had been taken from me twenty-three months ago. Also my wallet, watch, and cap.

"I've got the release order here. Hurry up, would you?"

They were expecting me to change right there so I did. When I put my trousers on they were too big in the waist.

"I don't want to sound ungrateful," I said, "but the concert is tonight and if there's any way—"

Three minutes later I was standing outside the wall. Not far away a church bell started to sound. I just stood there, smelling the air. Two kids rode by on bicycles, turning their heads to look at me.

I wondered if that had really been me back there, asking if I could stay, or some dope who just looked like me. I started down the road. As I walked I began to hum "Who's Sorry Now?"

THE SIX

THE RIFT WAS A TERRIBLE THING. IT WASN'T OVER something trivial and I didn't think that anything would ever be the same.

Almost from the beginning, we called ourselves the Six. We weren't the same age, didn't have the same backgrounds, but we came together when the town needed us.

The occasion was a fire that burned down three houses by the railroad tracks; the cause never was discovered. Really, they weren't much better than shacks but families lived in them—*less fortunate*, as my father said—with a bunch of kids in each. I was only sixteen when it happened but my mother had been urging me to get involved in the community, so when a notice went up for a woman's committee, I joined.

Seeing as it was serious work, I didn't expect to have such a good time. I remember how awkward I felt at that first meeting in the Methodist church basement, at least at the start. We were supposed to raise money for the lumber and shingles and nails and everything else the volunteer crew of men needed to build three new houses, and we agreed to hold a bunch of events — raffles, a cakewalk, a rummage sale.

After the big decisions were made the woman who was chairing the meeting, Harmony, said, "You all understand that this is just an excuse for us to eat sweets and dish the dirt." Everyone laughed and then the girls — that's what they always called themselves, never women — started chatting away. And somehow the work got finished, too.

Being the youngest, I didn't have much to say, at least not until Edna, who ran the free lending library out of her front parlour, asked me about myself, and everybody turned to listen. I said that I had just finished school and was helping my mother with my younger brothers and that I had a beau named Bertrand Katridge who I thought was going to propose to me. "Oooh!" they all moaned and then laughed and I couldn't tell if they were hopeful or sorry for me.

After the houses we took on other projects, such as distributing literature on milk homogenization, helping some of the widows in town, and sending parcels to the incarcerated. It was another year or two before we realized that we didn't always need a cause to get together and enjoy each other's company. We started to meet on Thursday evenings after chores, sometimes at Harmony's house, sometimes at Edna's or Alberta's. Once in a blue moon we went to the Good Times Restaurant and filled two tables and made so much noise we sounded like a hen house, the cook said.

I'm sure that our group was important to all of us, but I was learning what it meant to be a grown woman, and their example had a real influence on me. I learned that there wasn't just one way to think, or dress, or live. I saw what was needed to overcome tragedy, and that all of us were stronger than we thought. Like Lou-Anne, whose husband died cleaning his shotgun (or perhaps deliberately, it was whispered). Still, she needed us and the others showed me how to help. And as Alberta said, we'd all be in that position sooner or later, needing the others.

All of this is why the rift was so awful. Edna's only son volunteered for the army and three months later was in France and three days after that was presumed dead, his body never found. Such a terrible time it was for her, and after the memorial service we all just kept on visiting. One afternoon we happened to all be there, crammed into Edna's parlour, when Harmony said in almost an offhand way that it was a "stupid war" and a "waste of life." Edna looked up, shocked, and accused Harmony of saying that her son had died for nothing. And Harmony—who'd always been stubborn—got defensive and heated up, and finally Edna told her to leave the house and never return.

Afterwards the rest of us argued about who was in the wrong, but I knew only that I needed these women in my life. The war went on and more boys from around here got killed, and Lou-Anne, who had nurse's training, went overseas and worked in a hospital in England, and it seemed to me that the world was coming to an end.

Then came the armistice. Some of the young men came back, if not always whole, and Lou-Anne returned, too, looking older and sadder. We didn't have each other like we used to, didn't call ourselves the Six anymore. After a while I decided that maybe it was me who had to do something about it, rather than waiting for somebody else to fix things. I got the idea of doing something to remember Edna's son. I called Lou-Anne and Alberta and Norma together and also Harmony, who I practically had to drag over to my house. I proposed that we get a real town library built and name it after Edna's son, who used to help his mother lend out books when he was a boy. Everyone — even Harmony — thought it was a fine idea. Alberta took charge of procuring books while Lou-Anne and I would make a formal proposal to the town to donate the land. Alberta said that she would approach Mr. Carnegie, the millionaire, or rather his charitable organization, which funded library construction in cities all over.

But none of it could happen if Edna didn't agree. I took it upon myself to visit her, and I asked Harmony to come. There was some debate about whether bringing Harmony was such a good idea — well, there was a lot of debate — but in the end everyone agreed.

The next morning we walked to Edna's house and knocked on the door. I'd never seen Harmony look so nervous. Edna peeked at us through her curtains and then took her time letting us in. Two hours we sat with her, and more than half the time nobody said a word. But we got our idea across and finally Edna agreed to let us name the library after her son. That was really the hardest part. The town gave the land, not on the main street but a block north, and the Carnegie Foundation gave the funds. A two-storey library with a stone facade went up and it stands there today, still the most handsome building in town.

The building is used, for one reason or another, by just about everyone. On the second floor is a meeting room with lovely wainscotting and an arched window that is directly above the main entrance. Above the door to the meeting room is a small oak plaque with THE SIX carved in capital letters. That's because all of us gave personally for the decoration of the room. Young people sometimes wonder what it means, and if I'm within hearing, you can be sure that I always tell them.

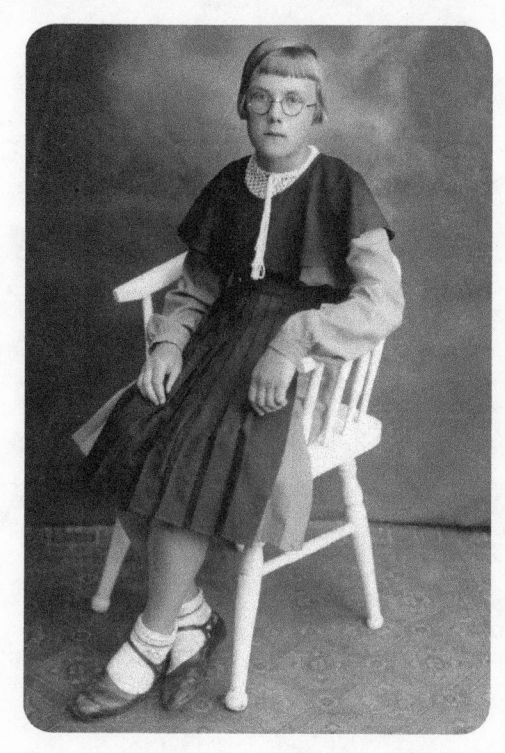

SUBVERSION

WHAT DO YOU SUPPOSE SHE'S THINKING, SITTING there?

How do I know? The best way to destroy this place, probably.

What are you talking about? She's a child. These accusations against her have to be exaggerated.

You've read the reports?

I've only had a chance to glance at them. Where is her latest report card?

At the very front of the file. You'll see—

Yes, yes, I can read perfectly well. What I see is that she got first in math, first in chemistry, first in biology. And she's captain of the chess team. But of course I knew that. The chess team is the pride of your school.

She *was* the captain. She's been removed from the team.

Why? Last year you won the provincials. The newspapers even wrote about her match. I remember something about sacrificing three pieces and deceiving her opponent.

A perfect example of her natural deviousness. In any case, I had no choice but to remove her. She was coaching the other teams.

I'm sorry?

Every Wednesday night. She organized it in some ice cream shop. Anyone could come and work through chess problems. The best players from the other schools were coming to learn from her.

And you asked her to stop?

Several times.

So?

She said that chess wasn't about winning. That it was about problem solving or some nonsense like that. When I threatened her with expulsion from the team, she just shrugged and said that she would prefer to continue her Wednesday nights and that she could always play chess in the park on Saturdays.

Impudence, eh? But let's not get sidetracked. Teaching chess isn't why we're here.

No, of course not. I hardly would have asked you to come from the board office for that.

Look how she sits without even fidgeting. I'd really like to know what's going on in that brain of hers.

Don't even try to figure her out. She's not normal. She's a freak—and a dangerous one.

All right, that's enough. Just give me the details.

Fine. It started when the head of the history department

decided to begin a new after-school club. He found it hard for a history club to compete with soccer, film appreciation, all that sort of thing. So he started a Patriotic Club where students could organize fireworks displays and skits about our great national events, etc. He had a good turnout at the first meeting, twenty-five kids or so.

Including her.

Yes. She didn't speak during the first couple of meetings. It was on the third that she made a suggestion.

She was rude, I suppose.

Not at all. She put up her hand and when called on she stood up and addressed the meeting quite properly. She suggested they rename themselves the Anti-Patriotic Club.

You aren't serious.

Of course the teacher should have cut her off right then and there. But he was too surprised to stop her from spouting subversion while the other students listened with wide eyes. Let's admit it, children are very impressionable when it comes to rhetoric against authority.

What did she say exactly?

That patriotism had been responsible for every war since Troy. She said that in a proper world there wouldn't be countries, or police, or passports at all. Or armies.

She impugned our soldiers?

Not our ordinary soldiers, our generals. And do you think the teacher stopped her then? As we speak, that teacher is on his way to one of our most isolated rural schools to teach kindergarten. But to go on, she said that their duty wasn't merely to those who lived within our borders, but to all of humanity. By all accounts everyone got excited, voiced agreement, stamped feet. They called out, "Yes, you're right!" and "Why aren't they teaching us this!" and the like. Immediately a committee was struck to organize a protest march calling for the end of competitive sports.

Oh, please!

Several students began composing an open letter demanding an end to all tests and grading. Somebody found a guitar in the cupboard and began to sing a folk song. Other issues got bandied about—vegetarianism, bicycles instead of cars, and, by the older students, sexual liberation. Only now did the teacher try to take control of the meeting, but the students ignored him, bursting from the room to begin disseminating their brilliant new ideas. By the next morning the entire school had been turned upside down. Students actually jeered during the national anthem.

Outrageous!

The zoo had been taken over by the animals. Nobody attended class. All the instruments in the music room were taken out without being signed for, only to be bashed on by kids who didn't even know how to play. The countries on the world map in the geography room were painted out and the words *One World* scrawled across. The secretaries fled, afraid for their lives. Some of the kids took over the office and used the mimeograph to produce a magazine with a cover photograph showing a naked—a naked ass.

And this girl? No doubt she was in the middle of it.

Not at all. She merely went to the school library and spent the day reading chess books. Fortunately, I managed to get control of the school the next morning. I locked the students in the classrooms and brought in their parents. I let them out only one at a time. Many of them cried, of course. We began a program in re-education. Only that girl hasn't agreed to participate.

The cheek! What did she say?

When we accused her of being a radical, she told us that she wasn't political at all and that really all she was interested in was chess. In fact she had spent her time working out alternatives to the famous 1932 grandmaster game between—

I don't care about that! Just look at her sitting there. Trying to look so innocent. I still can't fathom how a young girl could cause such an upheaval. Tell me, what do you propose we do?

I've been pondering that. She's bright, that's for certain, and I can't help thinking what an asset she would be if her ideals were only channelled in the right direction. And let's admit it, the system can always use a little reform, some tweaking here and there to raise people's enthusiasm. She needs to be made to understand. That's why I asked for you to come. I want you to go in and talk to her.

Me? I'm certainly not going to convince her of anything. We need to nip this in the bud. We can't have this spread to any other schools. You should go in there and tell her what's what.

But she has no respect for me. That's why I called you.

You'll just have to change that, won't you? Go on. I'll be observing everything.

Observing! Aren't you supposed to solve problems like this? But I understand. You're afraid of the girl.

Don't be ridiculous. If anyone is afraid, it's you who's shaking in your boots.

Well, I'm not going in.

And I'm not doing your job for you.

Suit yourself. Leave her there.

Come on, now. Go!

You go!

But look, she's getting up!

What is she doing?

She's knocking on the glass!

She can't even see us.

This is too big for me or you. We're going to have to go higher up.

Yes, yes, I absolutely agree. This will have to go to the top.

FATE

THE CAR WAS OLD BUT THE MECHANIC HAD GONE over it thoroughly and the trailer was brand spanking new. I was the first person to buy one, the dealer told me that. The money for it came from my uncle, who'd dropped dead at the age of forty-seven. That was the history of our family, the men dying young. My own father had made it to only thirty-five. What was I waiting for?

Mary Beth wasn't too pleased at first. For one thing, she was pregnant and in the nauseated phase. For another, our two boys were in school, not to mention they were an ill-behaved handful. But I promised her the experience of a lifetime. I said we'd be back a good couple of months before the baby was due. And when we got back I'd put up those new curtains she wanted.

"It isn't fair," she said. "How can I say no when you're likely to die three or four decades before me?"

I grabbed her and kissed her.

We left at the end of April, when the weather was starting to warm. The first days on the road we were all in good spirits. It wasn't long before we were seeing new views out the window, and even the boys were well-behaved. At night we'd pull into an empty field or a school playground and make our dinner on the portable oil stove. Then we'd lie on our bunks and sleep soundly. The fresh air had washed us clean. The miles stripped away our dull, old selves.

And then came the first tragedy.

I told the older boy, who was eleven and never listened, not to hold out the honey jar to that bear. But he insisted and I thought, well, how else is he going to learn. But the bear went too far and ate the boy. Not all of him, of course, but enough. I couldn't see explaining what happened to the local authorities so we dug a hole under some trees and buried him. I didn't have a bible with me so I read a few words from Dante instead.

Not surprisingly Mary Beth said, "May this bring you to your senses." But I told her that if we went back now our son's demise would be for nothing. That we'd be teaching our younger one a lesson in defeatism rather than determination. So we went on.

The weather became truly fine and the woods were beautiful. We bathed in streams. We ate fish caught with rod and reel. To be honest, all of us found it easier without the older boy and all the noise he made. Our younger one missed him but was glad for his baseball glove and sling-shot. He even got a squirrel and we made a stew out of it, pioneer style, although Mary Beth refused to skin the thing and I had to do it. Our son pinned its tail to his baseball cap.

I had brought with me some of the great books: not just Dante but Plato, Thucydides, Nietzsche. It had been part of a plan to embark on serious study along the way and so every night I read aloud while the others lay in their bunks. Generally they fell asleep within minutes, but I always continued for a good while. I believe the sound of my voice was soothing to them and I hoped that the thoughts of these great men would enter their dreams.

We reached the mountains. The roads were often in poor condition and sometimes the tires were only inches from the edge of a terrible precipice, yet no matter how loud my passengers pleaded I never failed to call up their courage. We got one flat that I patched and another that I replaced with the spare. It's funny how you think that you are in the clear just when you are in the greatest danger. It was on the other side of the mountains, as we were sighing with relief, that the second tragedy struck.

I told our younger son not to walk along the edge of the well. But like his brother, he would not listen. It was a very deep well and his screams came up to us for several long seconds before the splash. Then silence. There was no way for me to get down, as the rope on the bucket was fraying and looked less than reliable. All I could do was use a piece of coal to write some words on a wooden board: *RIP Jimmy*. And under that: *Attention! Contaminated Water.*

Of course my arguments for going on were just the same as before. I believe that Mary Beth was too stunned to argue. I trusted time to bring her back to her naturally buoyant self.

We came to an arid land, almost desert, with prickly bushes and blowing tumbleweed. Several times the car almost overheated and we had to wait it out. Mary Beth suffered from the heat most, especially on account of her being quite large by that point. The promise I'd made to get back home for the birth had been long forgotten.

One hot afternoon our car became surrounded by a herd of cattle heading in the other direction. Cowboys rode their horses on the perimeter of the herd but one of them made his way up to us. He tipped his hat and said that there were some mean bandits living in caves near there and that we would be better off turning around.

"Don't expect my husband to listen to reason," said Mary Beth. I couldn't help smiling when she said it.

The cowboy turned out to be right. Two days later, in the early hours of dawn, we were asleep in our bunks when a dozen ruffians surrounded the trailer. They threatened to light it on fire so we had no option but to emerge. They wore scarves over their faces. I asked what they wanted, concerned that they would find the remains of my uncle's money, which I had hidden in various compartments. But before any of them had a chance to answer, Mary Beth stepped forward.

She was even bigger now and no doubt due within the month. "This is no time for bravery," I said.

But she didn't listen. She went up to the nearest bandit on his horse and said, "Help me up."

"Mary Beth?" I said.

She didn't speak to me but took the proffered hand, got a foothold on the saddle, and slowly rose onto the back of the horse. To be accurate, it was almost more pony than horse.

"If we're going, let's go," she said to the bandit.

I admit to being bitter for several days, until finally I realized that it was probably for the best. Now I could make decisions without rancour. I could be more careful with my funds and stay longer on the road, perhaps indefinitely. At the next town with a garage I had the automobile and the trailer given a good once-over. The car needed an oil change, a new fan belt, and fresh break pads. The chassis of the trailer needed to be welded in a couple of spots. I got a new spare tire. Mary Beth's and the boys' clothes I sold to the general store. On a shelf was a beat-up copy of Shakespeare's plays and a small chess set. I bought them both.

I got back into the car and began to drive. Before long I had once again left human habitation behind. At night I would read aloud from *Othello* and then begin a game of chess, taking both sides. In the morning I would move on. Perhaps I'd have a heart attack behind the wheel, the way my father had died while at his streetcar conductor job, or while putting on my socks, like Uncle Dahlbert. It was an adventure in itself just to see how far I could go, and how long I would last before fate came to eat me, or drown me, or otherwise carry me away.

CHARISMA

M Y STEPHANIE HAS BEEN TAKING TAP FOREVER, or at least it seems that way. All those after-school classes and then the Christmas and spring shows. But so have a lot of the girls, and some boys too, especially since Rita took over the dance studio when Miss Tierney retired. Rita is just the most charismatic thing in the world. She moved here when she bought the studio, and frankly it's hard to understand what would make such a pretty and sophisticated girl come to a place like this. But ever since she started, the town has kind of gone dance crazy. Suddenly everybody wants to be Ginger or Fred. Even the adult classes are full. And in the school playground, instead of kids talking about TV shows or the latest hit song, they're showing each other the heel drop, the spank, the scuff, the paddle, the riff, the bear.

Of course Rita's demeanour and looks haven't hurt. And it's not as if the men in town haven't noticed. My own husband said she was just about as fresh as a peach pie. And she wears those cashmere sweaters and toreador pants with bare ankles and little dance slippers, and to be honest if I looked like her I'd do the same. Besides, it's hard to be annoyed at her when she's so nice, and she doesn't flirt with the fathers or show anyone special attention.

To be strictly honest I think this treating everyone exactly the same is one of her minor faults. It goes without saying that some children are naturally going to be more talented than others. And more dedicated as well. My Stephanie—well, there's no girl in town more devoted to those dance classes than her. All day long it's "Miss Rita says arms are as important as feet" and "Miss Rita says perfect execution without feeling is like dry toast without butter." She even insisted that I let her get her hair bobbed just like Rita so now it's as short as a boy's, and to be honest on Stephanie it doesn't look quite so flattering. But the point is how hard Stephanie has worked. She's gone to every one of Rita's extra classes. She had her father install a mirror in her room so she could watch herself practice, the way professional dancers do. That girl has poured her heart into it.

And now this contest. To be fair it wasn't Rita's idea. It was Morris Rittenworf's. He thought a dance competition would spur the children on to "excel themselves." Of course I've known the Rittenworfs forever and Anita is as sweet as honey but that Morris—well, anyone who's tried to buy a lawnmower from him knows how pushy he can be. And in my humble opinion the desire to win is not always the best motivation. But a lot of other parents jumped on the bandwagon, and then somebody suggested that it could be a fundraiser to help put a sprung floor in the school gymnasium where the recitals are always held, and of course Rita couldn't resist that idea, so it was decided then and there.

I wish Stephanie hadn't wanted to win so badly. I actually thought she was making herself sick with caring about it. And all that practicing! She got sore ankles and hips. At night she couldn't calm down enough to sleep. Half the tickets sold right away but then almost none did and rumour was that a whole bunch got given away to just anybody.

Between you and me, I think a lot of the audience came to see Rita open the program with a solo dance of her own, wearing that slinky black leotard. She got a few whistles along with the applause. Rita then welcomed everyone and reminded us that the most important thing was for the kids to "express themselves and feel the joy of movement." To which I said to myself, *Ha!*

Naturally I watched the other contestants with an eye to comparing them to my Stephanie. Marcy Marker dressed up as a hobo and played the harmonica while she danced. The twins, Lucy and Sally Korman, also twirled batons (were all these props even allowed?). Donald Berton sprinkled cornmeal on the stage and did a soft-shoe; the janitor had to come out and sweep before Stephanie came on. She danced better than I've ever seen her perform before. Her smile never wavered. Her arms never stopped moving. I got positively dizzy watching her. When she took her bow I could just see her beaming.

And then came the Gonzalez kids.

First of all, their mother, Maria, used to be a singer in a wedding band, which certainly gave her children an advantage. Second, maybe they were just kids but they had an unfair dose of charisma themselves. And third, they used steps that nobody around here had ever seen before. The guitar music began and they just stared at the audience a moment before stamping their feet and making us all jump. They swayed their hips, clapped their hands. Their lithe bodies moved like swans, or snakes, and their feet were deadly little machine guns. The boy spun his sister toward himself and away again. The look in his eyes — well, it could only be described as smouldering.

I hardly have to tell the results. Stephanie came in second but if she was disappointed she didn't show it. She looked a picture of happiness as Rita handed her a ten-dollar gift certificate to the studio along with a little trophy. I let her keep the trophy in her room but as for the certificate, I told her that it was time for a new hobby. My husband thought I was being hard on her but I let him know that his opinion on the matter was not wanted. Stephanie cried, but a couple of months later she made the school volleyball team.

As it turned out, the next year Rita moved back to the city and closed the studio. By then my Stephanie had already become best friends with the Gonzalez girl. She was over at our house all the time, a perfectly nice child. The brother started coming too, and he would always say hello and look at me with those eyes. I started to worry about him hanging around so much. And because I kept my eye on him, I missed what was going on altogether.

TINY HISTORY

SEPTEMBER 13, 2016

Shit, that's beautiful. Kev, are you looking at this?

One second.

Stop texting. This is the most incredible view I've ever seen.

There's no reception. What's up with that? Oh, wow, you're right. It's sick.

If everyone would please gather around, and be careful not to go beyond this sign. The rocks can be quite slippery. It is here that Oresta Collings walked on the night of May 13, 1901, after receiving a telegram stating that her fiancé had been killed in the Boer War. She had written a brief poem and left it up in her room in the house —

Where the hotel is now, right?

That's right. It's such a shame the house was torn down. That's the power of money for you. As some of you may know, Oresta did not publish a single poem in her lifetime. Her work was known only by her closest friends. It was her fiancé, Gilbert Winters, who first urged her to publish. He was a great support to her. She hadn't yet decided whether she wanted to publish — we know this from her letters — and then, despite her pleas, Winters went off to war. She received the telegram reporting his death and a few hours later wrote the poem that is now known by its first line — "I Am Lost." I think she truly loved Gilbert Winters, and felt that at last, at the age of thirty-five, she'd found someone who understood her. She came down the same path that we ourselves took. It was just before midnight and a full moon. And she threw herself or perhaps fell into the water, we'll never know for sure.

Did she put stones in her pocket or something?

It wasn't necessary. The currents here are very strong. It is believed that Oresta was almost immediately dashed against the largest outcropping. She had a significant gash on her head. Likely she was unconscious when she drowned, a small mercy. When you are ready please follow me back up the path. Feel free to take your time.

That's just so sad, eh, Kev? To think she stood right here. I guess every spot has its own tiny history.

If you ask me she had a screw loose, killing herself for some guy.

You mean if something happened to me you wouldn't feel like that? I don't mean actually doing it, but you wouldn't at least for a while feel like life wasn't worth living?

Don't start with the weird questions. I'm going to get a video of the waves hitting the rocks. I can post it back at the hotel.

Kevin, she said not to go any farther.

I've got good soles on these Docs. I've always been good at—shit, now my pants are soaked.

Serves you right. Don't be stupid for once, Kev. Just come back.

Just one more—oh, fuck! I can't believe—I dropped my phone. That phone is almost new. I've got all my photos from the trip...

I told you. And now you're really scaring me. Get back here.

All right, soon as I grab my phone. Before it washes away.

Remember what she said, those rocks are—Kevin! Oh Jesus. Kevin! Help! Somebody help!

JULY 9, 1983

Did I tell you, sis? That it would be a good spot?

You did. And it is. It takes my breath away. It's awe-inspiring. Dad would really have loved it here.

That's just what I said. He sailed past here once, I can't remember which race it was. A couple of miles out, of course.

Dad loved those races. Did he ever win?

Not once. I don't think he even came close. He just liked to be out on the water, to be in control but under pressure at the same time. It made him feel free.

I'm sure he was more comfortable dealing with his

crew than people on land. "Pull this, yank that." That was his ideal conversation.

He was going to sail a lot more, now that he finally had the time. I said that I might go with him sometimes. And then it came on so quickly, one moment he's the picture of health and the next—

Oh, I hate to think about it. He should have had more time.

I'll take the lid off. Do you want to do it?

Let's do it together. Are you okay there? I don't want either of us slipping.

I'm fine. Just be careful to keep it low so the ashes don't blow back on us. Do you want to say a few words?

I've said them all in my heart already.

All right. Here we go.

Goodbye, Dad.

AUGUST 24, 1969
Are you scared?

I'm not scared.

Then catch up.

Okay, okay! But Mom and Dad told us not to come down on our own. And I already got a soaker in my running shoe.

So? I've got two soakers—*I* don't care. And Mom and Dad are asleep in the tent. We won't tell them, okay? You said you wanted to come with me.

I know. But the rocks are hard on my feet. And the waves scare me.

Waves are fun. Here, if you really need to, crybaby, hold my hand.

I'm not a crybaby.

Don't squeeze so hard. The water isn't even that cold. We could just go in up to our knees.

It looks like it gets deeper over there. I can't see the bottom.

I know what we can do. We'll hop in together. And then the wave will lift us like we're surfing. It'll be fun.

I don't want to.

You *are* a crybaby.

If I do will you play with me after? Not here, back up at the top.

Okay, I'll count to three and then we'll jump. Are you ready?

Ready!

One...two...here we go...*three!*

NOVEMBER 4, 1942

Well, have you got him?

It's tricky, sir. The cords are still caught between the rocks.

Then cut him loose. Before he looks any worse, damn it. Who saw him come down?

Private Ricket saw him, sir.

Where's Ricket? Right. Tell me what you saw, Private.

He was coming down too fast, sir. There was something wrong with his chute, one side was kind of flapping. It wasn't slowing him down enough. I think he would have been all right if he'd gone straight into the water. But he hit one of the rocks.

Did you see the Hawker?

Came down in a spin, spewing black smoke. Broke up when it hit the surface.

Blast it. This is a bad time to lose a plane.

Funny thing, sir. I believe this is the place where Oresta Collings died.

Who?

The poet, sir. I was a graduate student before signing up. Her work was published just a few years ago. She's become quite the rage. In certain circles, I mean. In fact I carry a small volume—

I don't care about some poet, Private.

No, sir.

Here they come. Help haul him up, would you? I've got to file a report.

JUNE 11, 1877

It's lovely, Papa. Are we really going to live here?

In the summers we are. We're going to build a house right on the crest. I'm going to have a study and your mother will have a studio. And your own room will be at the very top. You'll have a wonderful view.

I think there will be terrific storms. Thunder and lightning and great crashing waves.

You are a little Romantic, darling.

And when it's clear and warm? Can we go swimming then?

No, it's very dangerous. There are powerful currents among the rocks. But there's a beach about a mile down. We'll go there. We can have picnics.

And I'm going to bring the notebook you gave me. See, Papa? I have it in my big pocket. I already wrote a poem. It's about sorrow.

That's a very grown-up topic.

I'm going to write another one about joy. You'll like that better.

Much better. You're a very smart girl to know your father so well. And after you've written it you can read it to your mother and me.

I've already got a first line. Can we stop here, up on the grass? And you can smoke your pipe.

That's a fine idea.

I'm going to be a real poet, you know.

I believe you, darling. I'm sure you are.

YOU SHOULD HAVE COME

I WAS MAD FOR THE THEATRE, AND IT WAS THIS MAD-ness that saved me. But it did not relieve me of the grief and guilt I felt over my sisters' deaths.

I had been a late, unexpected child, and my sisters were much older than me. And when our mother and father died they became, in effect, my parents. They thought we would be safer in the countryside and so we moved from our apartment to a small cottage on the outskirts of a village. I was eighteen. Hannah was angry with me for not leaving the country when I'd had a chance to obtain a visa. But I was acting in my first professional production, playing the role of the manservant in Turgenev's *A Month in the Country*, and refused to go. "Soon, soon," I kept saying. Gerta, as usual, played the peacemaker. "This isn't the time to argue," she said. "We need to be together. A family. We need to think of our dear parents and love one another."

"For God's sake, Gerta, cut it out," Hannah said.

Before the play's run was over the company had to let me and several others go or risk being shut down, and by then it was too late to leave. I continued to take the train into the city to see my friends, to drink wine and join in the reading of new scripts. I knew my sisters would say the city was too risky, that anyone might betray me, so I kept these visits to myself. Instead, I told them that I was going to the nearby forest to look for mushrooms, berries, and to fish—anything to supplement our meagre food supply. Of course they complained when I came home empty-handed.

On one of my trips a stagehand who let me watch rehearsals told me that I'd been denounced and that the theatre was no longer safe. Seething with bitterness, feeling that this catastrophe was terrible only because it was ruining my life, I took the train back to the village. Approaching the cottage, I saw two black automobiles pulled up on the dirt road. Figures in long leather jackets went to the door while others moved around the side of the house. Why had they come for us? Had it been my fault? I didn't know what to do. Should I run to the house and plead with them not to take my sisters? Surely they would just take all of us. And so I ran.

I headed back into the woods. I knew only the mile or two near our cottage but I kept going, avoiding any signs of human life. As it got dark I found a place, not a cave but a mere hollow in the earth from where a tree had fallen, pulling out the roots. I lay down. Every so often I heard a sharp sound in the distance; it reminded me of the strange noise at the end of *The Cherry Orchard*.

For three months I stayed in the forest. Never in that time did I have enough food or feel that I was safe. Twice I met up with other people who were also hiding, but I decided it was better to remain alone. Autumn came and it rained and grew cold. Food became almost impossible to find. After three days with nothing to eat I became delirious. I found a road and began to walk. At the first house I came to I knocked on the door, hardly able to keep standing. The door was opened by a small, balding man in a jacket and tie. He did not ask my name but brought me in and gave me a bowl of soup and bread. Then he showed me to a tiny room at the back of the house where there was a straw-filled mattress and a blanket. I lay down and slept.

The man was a professor of law who was no longer allowed to teach or practice because of certain articles he had published. He did not ask me to hide. I worked at odd jobs for him, rebuilding the front porch, plastering the rooms, hoeing the vegetable garden. He had a good library that I was welcome to use. I read books of history, science, and poetry. I moved on only when I felt that my presence was putting him at too great a risk.

And so I lived, sometimes on my own, sometimes with others or with help, until the end of the war. I had no family left. I couldn't see staying in that country and so, after many letters and the issuing of documents, I got on a ship and left for the "New World."

I learned English and went to university, where I began to act in plays again. The approach to theatre was much different and, I thought, much less serious, but I adapted. I got my first professional jobs and then began to direct. I specialized in Strindberg, Ibsen, and of course Chekhov. The better theatres had an appreciation for European artists or, should I say more frankly, a foolish but useful reverence. I also taught at the university.

There were, of course, women, but none was more important than the others until one evening at a closing-night party. I watched a woman setting out food on a tray—a real job, feeding people, I thought. We began to go out, became a couple, and after she got pregnant we married. We had two daughters, beautiful, smart, stubborn little girls named in honour of Hannah and Gertie. Sometimes at bedtime they would ask me about my sisters and I would say, "Oh that Hannah, she was wonderful and strong and difficult and thought she knew what was best for me. You know what? Probably she was right. And Gerta, sweet Gerta, she was very sensitive. Raised voices, arguing, disturbed her soul." I did not tell them what had happened to their aunts; that could wait until they were older.

One evening I came home exhausted from a difficult rehearsal. We had dinner, read to the girls, put them to bed. Before long we were asleep ourselves. Then the telephone rang. It was four in the morning. A harsh voice in the old language said, "Is that you? It's your sister Hannah."

"What? Hannah?"

"And here is Gerta beside me. It took us all these years to find you. You shouldn't have changed your name. We are coming to visit and will arrive in one week."

I had hardly said a word before the line went dead. My wife stirred beside me, saying, "Who was that? One of your neurotic actors?"

"No," I said. "It was my sister. Hannah."

She sat up. "What do you mean?"

"She's alive."

"I can't believe it."

"Yes. And my sister Gerta, too. It was Hannah's voice, I'd forgotten it. How have they been alive all these years without my knowing? Living in Europe still, one day after another."

"How old are they now?"

"Let me think. Fifty-three and fifty-five. They're coming here next week."

"Oh my God, that is so wonderful. How do you feel?"

I couldn't answer because I didn't know.

We didn't own a car so a week later we all took the bus to the airport. The girls had a hundred questions that I couldn't answer. I checked the arrivals board and then stood at the big window while Hannah and Gertie—the little ones—held my hands. Planes took off and landed. At last one taxied to the gate below us. The plane sat on the tarmac for perhaps fifteen minutes before the door opened and passengers began coming down the stairs. None of them looked as if they could be my sisters. The final passenger emerged, or so it seemed, for there was a long pause and then two women came hesitantly out and made their way slowly down the steps. At the bottom one took the arm of the other. I easily recognized them—Hannah the tall one but now with a limp, Gerta looking broader but with her hair in just the style it had always been.

"There they are," I said, and the girls began to wave, hesitantly and then almost frantically. My sisters didn't see us, at least not at first, and when they finally spotted us they didn't wave back but kept walking. Now we hurried down to the floor below and waited outside the door, waited what seemed an age before they finally came out, followed by a porter with two ancient trunks on a luggage cart.

My wife kept hold of the girls as we approached. "My sisters, my dear sisters," I said in the old language, holding out my arms.

Hannah came forward and slapped my cheek.

"You should have come back for us."

"Stop it, Hannah," Gerta said. "Here's our brother, our little brother. Isn't it wonderful?"

"Of course it is," Hannah said and hugged me hard. Gerta kissed my wife and they both began to cry. Then Hannah leaned down. I thought that the children would be afraid of her, but they weren't. They ran right into her arms.

INVISIBLE

HIM: I was in love with her sister. She was beautiful and mysterious, and I thought that I might be the answer to her unhappiness. I didn't see this as arrogance but as a kind of humility. And what did I do about it? Nothing. I didn't have the courage, or perhaps just the experience. And then she was gone.

HER: What is every girl's model of a married couple? Her own parents. I had the example of two people who could not even find the energy to hate one another. Instead, what they felt looked merely like distaste. Perhaps they enjoyed the sarcasm. I remember when I was a teenager I wished that they would both have affairs and just shut up for a while. But I'm sure neither of them did, and not because of a secret fondness for one another or even loyalty. I'm sure they'd become too twisted for anyone to want them.

HIM: My father brought me up. My mother died giving birth to me and from the earliest age I felt this fact as both guilt and responsibility. I didn't argue when my father said that nothing was more important than my studies. He was a plumber and put in extra hours on weekends and nights—he was always on call. A good university was expensive and he needed to save for me. In the end, though, I got a full scholarship and didn't need the money.

HER: I was the invisible one. People would look right through me. It was my sister they always noticed—she was beautiful and willowy, and she never really looked at anyone directly because she was always gazing inward. This disturbed and attracted people. And yet every once in a while she would take notice of me. I would wake in the night to find she had crawled into my bed and wrapped her arms around me. Possibly she was cold; she was almost always cold. Other times she might braid my hair, and she would ask me the sorts of questions adults asked—what I liked at school, did I have a crush on any boys.

Every few months came another crisis and there would be doctors, psychiatrists, nutritionists, hospitals. More than once my parents forgot to leave me a note, or a meal. Once they left me waiting at a street corner, our meeting place after my flute lesson. I waited almost an hour and then walked home in the growing dark. A man started to follow me. I got scared and finally turned around and yelled at him until he went away. I walked the rest of the way home crying.

But they didn't forget me the day she died. When I came home from school they were sitting on the sofa, waiting to tell me. It wasn't necessary for them to say anything.

HIM: Our parents were old friends, so of course my father felt obliged to visit frequently during the period of mourning. He took me with him when I was free, for by then I was in my first year of university. (In the sciences, biology and chemistry, there is a lot of work.) Her parents were stricken. They no longer made the sarcastic remarks to each other that everyone was used to hearing. But they couldn't help each other, either, even I could see that.

And then there was the younger sister. People paid lip service, they took her hand and asked how she was holding up but took no real notice of her. At least that's what I thought. I'd had time to think about my earlier feelings for the older one and now saw them as a sort of narcissistic fantasy. I vowed not to be so naive about myself again.

HER: I didn't talk about my sister to anyone, except the school counsellor because I had to. I told her what she wanted to hear, but was any of it true? Not in the way I said, because it was far worse. At first I thought there was a big hole in me, an emptiness that could never be filled. But slowly I realized it wasn't empty because the whole universe was pouring into me.

Visitors came. They brought casseroles, salads. I sat in a chair and smiled and didn't hear my own voice. He came with his father. I didn't know him well, although I'd seen him now and again for years, ever since we were both young. He was two years older than me. Of course I knew that he had been infatuated with my sister. In all those years I don't think he ever talked to me other than to say hello just to be polite.

And then one afternoon, when the house was quiet, he said, "Shall we play something?" We had a pile of all the usual board games. They'd sat on a shelf beneath the end table for years, unused.

HIM: I could only imagine how painful and yet deadly boring these visits were for her. It wasn't that I liked games; in fact I'd always been bad at them, which was strange considering my math skills. She looked at me and said, "Why not?" and we just grabbed the first box and began to set up the board. I watched her play, watched her eyes and the slight movement of her mouth. She was quick-witted and also wanted to win. I decided not to let her, but I lost anyway.

HER: Even after the mourning period was over, he would come with his father. And we would pick a game at random and play and talk in low voices. He really wasn't very good at any game. He spoke slowly, thoughtfully, and if he made a joke it was so understated that I didn't get it for a moment. But when I did, I laughed. One day I asked myself whether he was handsome. I couldn't make up my mind so I decided that he was.

HIM: I began to say to my father, "Do you think we should pay a visit?" And when he decided that it was time to stop, that the family needed to be left alone, I began to go by myself.

HER: When spring came he asked if I wanted to take a walk. And the next week he asked if I wanted to go out with him and some of his friends from university. I wasn't interested in the boys in my grade so I said sure. We went to a café where we drank strong coffee and talked about what they were studying. There were heated arguments about politics and music and novels. I began to read the books they talked about so that I could join in. They treated me like an adult. They agreed with me or told me I was absolutely wrong or called me an *idealist*.

He always listened to me and thought before replying. I could see that he wasn't afraid to be swayed by my point of view. One day a friend asked him about his studies. He was going to have to focus exclusively on the sciences next year if he wanted to go into research. He would even have to dissect a cadaver.

"You'll be able to see into the human heart," someone joked.

"The heart is just a muscle," I said.

HIM: "The heart is just a muscle," she said.

"Yes," I responded, "but an important one."

HER: He formally asked me out. Over time we became

a couple, but we still went out with his friends. I began university and became preoccupied with my own studies. But we always had time for each other. We talked about my parents, and his father. We knew that we would have to find our own way.

A year went by, another started. And then I waited for him to ask me, worrying about his tendency to be passive, to hope rather than do. But if he couldn't find the courage, I thought, then to hell with him!

HIM: I went to her door. I'd never been so nervous in my life. Despite knowing her so well, I couldn't be sure of her answer. And then she opened the door and I looked into her eyes and couldn't speak. A plane appeared overhead, on its way to the airport. I waited for it to pass, and then still I couldn't get a word out.

HER: I said, "I already know the question, but you still have to ask."

HIM: I laughed. And I asked her. And when she answered I told myself not ever to forget what I felt at that moment.

HER: I said, "I want a simple wedding. And a nice picture."

WHERE WE ARE NOW

I T HAS NOT BEEN EASY TO TRACK DOWN MY FORMER classmates, all these years later. Some, of course, I have continued to be acquainted with into adulthood. Others I have heard about through relatives. Some have made return visits (occasionally in a casket). I have come across articles in newspapers. Here, then, is a record of what has happened to us.

Elizabeth Ghero. Married the third son of the farm family next to her own. Bore seven children, raised prize chickens, put her sister into the county mental institution, buried her husband and remains still in the house, although the fields around her have gone to grass.

Alice Bailey. A class favourite, she was known for her fine sewing and became a seamstress with a fitting room above the lawyer's office. Married classmate Lymon Young who became a drinker, unable to hold down a job, and who emptied their cigar box of savings before getting on an eastbound train never to return. Seven years later Alice was able to have him declared legally dead, and she married another classmate, Lloyd Carley, even though he'd had polio and walks with crutches. Alice remains the best seamstress for eighty miles.

Henry Read. Struck by lightning at age seventeen while walking home from a rained-out baseball game. None the worse except for a white streak in his hair, he later became the well-known senator Henry "Lightning" Read, only to have his reputation tarnished by the Gorham Bridge scandal, about which he maintains his innocence.

Daniel Zorn. Died of the influenza.

Hilary Wright. Died of the influenza.

Donald Martin. Died of the influenza.

Celery Tompkins. Another farmer's wife, with twelve children (all surviving), grown senile now and living with the family of the second oldest, where she sits in a rocker on the porch and every so often says, "Never had a minute to myself, never had a minute."

Paul Buchanon. A wild boy who preferred hunting and fishing and trapping to book learning, he left school early and lived in a shack in the woods. One winter got his own foot caught in an iron trap he was setting and had to saw it off, afterwards packing the bloody stump with snow so he could drag himself the seven miles to town. Didn't change his life much.

Chancey Darling. Agricultural college, then an insurance job in which he spent his time trying to deny the compensation claims of farmers. He was the first person to drive an automobile along the town's main street. He parked the car in front of Matilda's Home Cooking for a piece of lemon meringue pie and when he came out again discovered that someone had shat on the driver's seat.

Matilda Oswin. Opened her own restaurant (see above) and then partnered with a businessman from the east to sell jars of jellied pig's feet using her recipe. Everyone said he would swindle her out of every last penny, but she is now the richest person in town and living in a mansion up on Norgate Hill. As a "companion" she took in another classmate, Dorothy Hall, known for her extreme shyness, and what the two of them get up to is nobody's business.

Milton Phar. Joined the army, killed at Verdun.

Walter Lowry. Joined the army, killed at the Somme.

Derek Enderby. Joined the army, survived, opened a tavern called Three Friends where he still tends bar.

Margo Nott. The oldest girl in the school, and known for being deeply religious. Surprised everyone by running off with the photographer who took the class picture. Her mama cried for a week while her father went looking for her. But when he found them (asleep in a hotel room), the "deed" was done. She and the photographer opened a studio in Chicago and, due to the World Exhibition, were very successful for several years until the Depression ruined the business.

William Lintz. Killed by a horse at age thirty-two.

Augustus Norham. Became the town's telegraph operator. One morning an overheard piece of gossip alerted him to the illicit relationship between his wife and a former classmate, Luke Tasnig. Left his post, found Luke having a piece of lemon meringue pie at Matilda's Home Cooking, and shot him in the head. Miraculously Luke survived. Augustus was convicted of attempted murder and served three years in the penitentiary. During that time he began to write Western novels, one of which was turned into a moving picture starring Ward Bond.

Luke Tasnig. After surviving a pistol wound to the head (see above), he became a Methodist preacher. Continues to preach at tent revivals.

Georgina Osborne. Moved, if rumours are to be believed, to Peru.

Robert Horne. Became a lawyer, then a judge. Gave Augustus Norham his lenient sentence, some say because Justice Horne had been picked on after school by Luke Tasnig.

Theodore Smith. Remembered in school for screeching on a fiddle whenever he got a chance, he became an energetic musician, often playing for dances. As a member of Smith's Sodbusters he found fame as a radio performer, also recording a number of 78 records. He eventually returned to farming but will still pick up his fiddle if anyone asks.

Blanche Higart. Married classmate Lawrence Baldwin who went to work at the distillery. Blanche had three boys, all of whom enlisted in the second great war. The eldest was lost to a U-boat while crossing the English Channel. The middle one died in the Battle of the Java Sea, and the third on the beach at Normandy. Blanche and Lawrence considered their life over, but then Blanche — her hair by then completely grey — became pregnant and gave birth to a daughter.

The histories of the rest are still unknown, classmates spread far and wide in this great world of ours. I hope to publish further updates in the future, at least until I myself am no longer capable of holding a pen or writing a coherent sentence, or when my own candle has burned to the end. And yet when we are gone, our children and their children will go on. All we can do is hope that the memory of our own time here on earth will be kept alight for a little while.

ACKNOWLEDGEMENTS

My great thanks to Sarah MacLachlan for her continuing support. To Janice Zawerbny for saying yes. To Melanie Little, for being a writer's dream of an editor. And to absolutely everyone at Anansi.

Thanks also to Rebecca Comay for being the first, best reader, and to Sophie Fagan and Yoyo Comay-Newman for sampling and giving their thumbs up.

Last, I humbly acknowledge and thank the unknown photographers and their subjects.

AUTHOR PHOTOGRAPH: © MARK RAYNES ROBERTS

CARY FAGAN has written several critically acclaimed books, including *A Bird's Eye*, finalist for the Rogers Writers' Trust Fiction Prize; *My Life Among the Apes*, long-listed for the Scotiabank Giller Prize; *Valentine's Fall*, finalist for the Toronto Book Award. He has also written many popular books for children, for which he has won the Vicki Metcalf Award for Children's Literature and the Marilyn Baillie Picture Book Award. He lives in Toronto.